Praise for *The Violent Season*

"As poignant as it is creepy...this book asks what we do when others won't listen to our stories of survival."

—*Booklist*

"A complicated blend of mystery and angst."

—*School Library Journal*

"Claustrophobic and intriguing...a novel that will keep you hooked all the way"

—*The Nerd Daily*

"Sure to leave readers unsettled, unsatisfied, and demystified... read if you dare."

—*The Tempest*

Also by Sara Walters
The Violent Season

MISSING DEAD GIRLS

MISSING DEAD GIRLS

SARA WALTERS

 sourcebooks
fire

Copyright © 2023 by Sara Walters
Cover and internal design © 2023 by Sourcebooks
Cover design by Maggie Edkins
Cover images © by Reilika Landen/Arcangel Images
Sourcebooks and the colophon are registered trademarks of Sourcebooks.

The characters and events portrayed in this book are fictitious or are used fictitiously. Any similarity to real persons, living or dead, is purely coincidental and not intended by the author.

All brand names and product names used in this book are trademarks, registered trademarks, or trade names of their respective holders. Sourcebooks is not associated with any product or vendor in this book.

Published by Sourcebooks Fire, an imprint of Sourcebooks
P.O. Box 4410, Naperville, Illinois 60567–4410
(630) 961-3900
sourcebooks.com

Cataloging-in-Publication data is on file with the Library of Congress.

Printed and bound in Canada.
MBP 10 9 8 7 6 5 4 3 2 1

This one's for me.

I didn't kill Madison Frank. But there was a picture of her body on my phone screen—on everyone's phone screen. She was broken like a porcelain doll dropped from a flight of stairs. Blood dripping from the corner of her open mouth.

The entire school hallway was filled with a symphony of phone alerts and rings, screens lighting up with the sickening twist of blond and red. And every eye turned to me.

They were looking at me because the message was sent from an account under my name. They were looking at me because the photo was followed by a text.

TILLIE GRAY KILLED MADISON FRANK.

Someone screamed. It cut through the symphony, silencing it.

My pulse was thudding in my ears. I felt a match strike in the center of my chest, burning through my rib cage.

Beside me, the door to the main office swung open and the principal and a group of administrators spilled into the hallway followed by the school resource officer.

His hand rested on his holstered gun, and in that moment, I wished he'd fire it.

"Tillie," Principal Vaughn spoke gently, like she was talking down a jumper. "You need to come with us."

I wished for a fire. I wished for the whole place to go up in flames, taking me and all my secrets with it.

A girl made of ash. A ghost.

A killer.

Chapter One

Lottie Southerland was pretending to drown again.

I watched her from the lifeguard stand, blinking behind my sunglasses. Her head dipped under the water, then came back up. She gasped for air, thrashing her arms. I smacked my stale gum and blew a bubble.

Lottie finally set her feet down in the three-foot-deep water, glaring at me.

"Weren't you going to *help* me?"

My bubble popped, and I lazily pushed the gum back into my mouth. I shrugged.

"Weren't you being a little faker?"

Lottie stuck her tongue out at me. I stuck mine out, flashing my middle finger. She turned and splashed away, kicking water in my direction.

The kids in this town were insufferable. They showed up at the club with their nannies and inattentive mothers, who ignored them while they pissed in the pool and barfed undigested frozen Snickers bars on the sand of the volley-ball courts. They took swimming lessons in the mornings and came back after lunch for a few hours of screaming and ignoring my whistle. Lottie was the worst of them. When I started a few weeks ago, I'd fallen for her fake drowning act a few times and dragged her stupid nine-year-old living corpse out of the shallow end when she spit water in my face and erupted into laughter.

Lottie's nanny, some Temple University student who was home for the summer, would barely glance up from her phone.

"You get used to her bullshit," she'd told me after the third fake rescue attempt. She shouldered a Saint Laurent bag that I'd seen her leave sitting in a puddle of pool water.

"Just ignore her next time."

Back in Philly, ignoring a girl usually led to the worst kind of things. *Just ignore her while she screams for help.* Sure, I'd thought. Easy enough for Some Girl Who Goes to Temple to say.

But now, weeks later, Lottie could kill someone in front of me and I would ignore her. Nothing I haven't seen before.

———

I took the summer job only so my mother would untangle the barbed wire she had wrapped around my very existence and breathe without her watching me. Since we'd left Philly, she'd been hovering—in doorways, in the chair across the dinner table after we'd finished eating, in the front window while I pulled my bike out of the garage. I wanted to swat her away like a gnat buzzing in my ear, but I knew she was only trying to love me. She was only making sure I knew that she did. After everything.

I tried to imagine her at eighteen, barely a year older than I was now, with a sleeping baby tucked into her zipped-up hoodie while she filled out college applications. I tried to imagine the weight of it, how heavy it was to keep someone alive when you didn't even know how to file your own taxes. Whenever she annoyed me, I went there in my head, sitting at that kitchen counter in my grandmother's house beside my eighteen-year-old mother cradling one-month-old me, and reminded myself that being her burden was a choice I had to actively make. I didn't have to choose it, but I did, too many times. And there she would be, in my bedroom doorway, tucking a lock of her short black bob behind one ear and eyeing me like I was a bomb, poised to explode at any moment. A daughter made of fire and smoke.

I blew the long whistle to signal adult swim, and a collective groan emanated from the kids in the pool as moms and nannies slid into the water with their floats. It was my break, so I hopped down from the lifeguard stand and swung my whistle lanyard around my finger, flip-flops smacking on the concrete as I made my way to the snack bar.

Halfway across the pool deck, Lottie approached me, her lips purple from the Popsicle she was eating, an overexaggerated look of disgust on her face.

"*You're* gonna get fired, ya know," she taunted, sticky purple melting down her fingers. "*I'll* tell my mom on you."

I feigned interest and concern, lifting my eyebrows at her.

"Me? Fired? From this absolute paradise of employment? Aw, man," I snapped my fingers. "What'll I do then?"

Before she could open her stupid purple mouth again, I blew my whistle sharply. She flinched and covered her ears, dropping her Popsicle. I knew I was grinning, even as Lottie stared at me slack-jawed and curled her small hands into fists at her hips.

"No food on the deck." I said, swinging my whistle again and walking toward the snack bar. Lottie stomped off behind me.

The snack bar at the club wasn't like the hot dog carts outside the neighborhood public pool in Philly, where we'd grab syrupy snow cones. The snack bar was less a snack bar and more an *actual* bar manned by one pretty pool boy or another. It usually rotated between Jackson and Liam, who were always dressed in navy-blue Westshore Country Club polos and khaki shorts.

Jackson was twenty-two, and I'd occasionally catch him

staying after his shift to shoot the shit with the golf caddies in the club's main bar, throwing back Heinekens and eating the free bar nuts. He was born and raised in Willow Creek, which he'd mentioned during one of my first afternoons at the country club, before the pool had officially opened for the season. He'd been standing behind the pool deck bar, dark hair smoothed back and thick shoulders hunched lazily.

"This place is like a black hole," he'd said, endlessly drying a fully dry glass with a bar towel. "Even when you think you're out, it sucks you back in."

Later I learned from the gossipy club waitresses that his pessimism was due to being forced back to Willow Creek by circumstance. He'd lost his server job in Harrisburg after he got caught selling coke out of the restaurant's parking lot and had to move back home. Or so they said.

I still thought there was some merit to his angst. Willow Creek seemed like one of those towns that sank its dull teeth into you and locked its jaw.

—————

Liam was eighteen, fresh out of Willow Creek High School and practically foaming at the mouth to get out of town. Penn State was waiting for him in the fall, complete with frat parties and keg stands, or so I imagined. He looked the type. He had a head full of loose honey-blond curls and the kind of tall, lean stature that turned the nannies and moms all dreamy eyed. He was always tossing his hair out of his eyes and flashing his white smile at the club ladies, and I would try to imagine him in braces or with acne, or with any kind of awkward imperfection to humanize him. He was at least relatively normal otherwise. He talked to me like I was a person, something I wasn't used to from people on this side of Willow Creek. His family were club members—they had a big house in the rich neighborhood in the north end of town—but when I asked Liam why he chose to waste his last high school summer working here, he shrugged.

"Nothing comes without a price," he'd told me, pushing his curls back with one hand. "Especially not shit from my parents. I'd rather not pay it."

That day, it was Liam behind the bar. He saw me coming and shot me a finger gun before setting a plastic cup on the bar and filling it with ice, 7 Up, and a splash of grenadine. As I stepped up to the bar, he dropped two maraschino cherries into the drink and slid it over to me. I pushed my sunglasses to the top of my head, and then dropped my elbows onto the bar with a loud sigh.

"That bad?" Liam asked, chuckling. I made a face and took a sip of my drink, glancing around to see if any club moms were within earshot.

"I swear to fucking God," I said, voice low. "Some of the people here make me wonder if straight white people deserve rights."

"Hmm... I think that's been up for debate for a while. Leaning toward maybe not."

I lifted my drink to cheers his words and took a long sip. I looked around again, scoping out the people gathered under the pool cabanas they could rent. I saw a group of girls draped over the chaise longues underneath the nearest cabana, a set of BMW keys spilling from one of their designer tote bags.

I locked eyes with a blond in the middle chaise. Her hair fell almost to her elbows, cat-eye sunglasses perched on top of her head. She wore a black bikini that tied behind her neck and sat low on her hips. She had one leg bent as she leaned back on the chaise, a queen surveying her kingdom. I'd seen her there before, always flanked by a handful of other impossibly beautiful girls. They were the kind of beautiful that felt like a threat. A razor blade hidden inside a tube of red lipstick.

She looked at me for a beat too long, and I felt my insides twist. It was as if she knew me, even though I knew she didn't. It still made my pulse jump.

"Madison Frank." Liam said.

His voice made me break eye contact with her.

"Huh?"

He leaned his elbows on the bar and nodded toward the blond.

"That's Maddie Frank. She lives a few houses down from me. You'll probably see her here most days in the summer."

I looked back at Maddie.

She was the embodiment of what I imagined all the girls

from the north end looked like—a mirage of long limbs and tan skin and a smattering of freckles on her cheeks and nose that looked like they'd been individually and strategically placed. The sort of girl who men used to start wars over. Back in Philly, I'd fought a girl like that in the school parking lot.

I had been so angry back then. Sometimes, I still was.

Maddie caught me looking at her again, and this time she lifted an eyebrow, one side of her mouth turning up into a smile.

My neck prickled with heat.

"I wouldn't." Liam's voice brought my eyes back to him.

"Hm? What?"

"Maddie. I wouldn't."

My neck grew even hotter, and I took a long sip of my drink while he watched me, half amused.

"You wouldn't what," I said.

"I wouldn't get involved," he said. He glanced over at Maddie. "Her and her friends? All they do is chew girls up and spit them out. You know, fake a friendship, and then demolish them until they barely wanna show their face at school again."

I tried to imagine this, that pride of lionesses draped over those chaise longues, enticing some pretty girl to trust them, only to go for her throat once she was close enough. Killing for sport, not sustenance.

"Yeah, I know girls like that," I said under my breath, remembering the sharp sting of red-polished fingernails digging into my arm. I knew too well the damage girls could do to each other. Especially girls who looked like Maddie. All that power in their pretty.

But still. I kind of wanted to know what her shampoo smelled like.

My shift ended at three. I climbed down from the lifeguard stand and tossed the foam rescue tube to Gigi as she came to take over.

"Save anyone today, Til?"

Gigi's real name was Ji-young, but she went by Gigi because she got tired of white people mispronouncing it, as she'd told me with a shrug on my first day. Her parents were both first-generation Korean Americans, and sometimes I'd listen to her talking on the phone with them during swim breaks, her home language sounding like a poem.

"I decided to let people be independent and work on saving themselves today."

Gigi tossed the rescue tube up to the chair, nodding.

"Good call. These people could stand to do a thing or two for themselves, for once."

I waved over my shoulder at her as I walked off to grab my things from the lifeguard office—or what we called an office. It was really a closet-sized room by the exit with member records and medical supplies stacked along the walls, crowding an ancient desktop computer at a cluttered desk. In one corner, the duty guards piled our stuff. I pulled my black cotton shorts over my red one-piece, throwing the strap of my bag over my shoulder. As I passed the bar to leave, I waved to Liam, but my gaze strayed to the cabana where Madison Frank had been with her friends. It was empty.

Out front, I knelt by the bike rack to undo my lock, cursing the fact that I had to ride the miles to the country club and back home every day if Mom wasn't off work to pick me up. My mom could probably afford to help me get a car, but after Philly, I knew she dreaded the idea of me having so much freedom. So much scared her now.

My lock was jammed. I tugged hard on it, cursing. I looked closer. The rust I'd been ignoring had probably gotten it stuck. I stood, landing a swift kick against the rack.

"Fuck."

"Looks like you've got yourself in a predicament."

The voice came from behind me. I turned to find its source. Madison Frank was leaning against one of the concrete pillars outside the pool entrance. She'd put a macramé black kimono over her bikini. An expensive-looking bag dangled lazily from one hand.

I was suddenly aware of my sun-flushed cheeks, of the wisps of hair that were stuck to the sweat on the back of my neck. She peered at me from behind a pair of oversized, sunglasses that she then pushed up into her hair. She pulled a toke from the tiny joint pinched between her fingers, then stubbed it out carefully on the concrete pillar before she tucked it into a pocket inside her bag. Her nails were painted black except for her middle fingers—those were bright red. She exhaled smoke as she approached me.

"Tillie, right?"

Hearing my name come out of her mouth caught me off guard. It took me a second too long to remember it was mine.

"Yeah. How—"

"Your name's on the duty board."

"You looked at the duty board to find out my name?" I asked, surprising even myself with the amused accusation. I raised both eyebrows at her.

"You know my name already, don't you?" She responded, matching my tone.

I didn't say anything. She knew I knew. And she looked so satisfied about it.

"Do you want a ride?"

She pulled out her keys, nodding toward the midnight-blue BMW X1 parked in one of the front spots.

I wished I could read her. She was hieroglyphics. A collection of pretty pictures I was trying, frantically, to assemble into meaning in my head. What did she want from me? Why did she give a fuck if I needed a ride?

Had she been standing there, waiting for me?

I remembered Liam's warning. But Madison's lips split into an expectant smile as she shook her car keys, and for a second, I forgot Liam existed. Forgot I existed.

"Sure. Yeah. Yes."

Chapter Two

Madison threw her bag on the back seat and rolled down all the windows. The interior of the small SUV was immaculate, and I figured it was relatively new. Aside from the few empty Red Bull cans in the front console and door pockets and the loose scrunchies and hair ties scattered around the passenger floor, I would have thought she'd driven it to the pool from the sales lot.

The car's computer system synced instantly with Madison's phone, and she turned up the volume as her playlist resumed in the middle of an Empire of the Sun and Wiz Khalifa song. I tried not to watch her too closely, but her magnetism only felt stronger now that I was close to her. I could smell the soft coconut and lime scent of her sunscreen.

She put the car in reverse and backed out, barely checking her backup camera and swinging her wheel around and putting the car in drive to speed out of the parking lot. The wind blew warmly through the open car windows, and her hair caught in the breeze. Madison turned the volume up again. As she went fifty down Country Club Boulevard, I realized that I hadn't told her where I lived.

"Why'd you move to Willow Creek?"

Madison was half yelling over the music and the open window. I dug my fingers into my palm, calming the sudden beating of my pulse. No one here was supposed to know. I wanted it to stay that way.

"My mom's job. She's a nurse."

Madison glanced at me as she drove. Even from behind her sunglasses, I could see doubt in her eyes. But she smiled and nodded, looking back at the road just in time to brake at the red light at Country Club and Westshore. Going left would take us to the south end, where I lived, and going right would keep us here in the north end and toward Madison's neighborhood.

"You wanna come over?" she asked, as if I'd been thinking out loud. "My parents are both out of town, and my friends are boring."

Her offer should have raised a thousand red flags. Giving me a ride was strange enough. Asking me to come over without knowing me at all made me skeptical.

Madison glanced at me, letting out a laugh at my expression.

"C'mon. Dude, I'm not gonna murder you or something."

I studied her face before I looked at the clock in the center console. My mom wouldn't be off her shift until ten. I had about six hours before I had to be back at the house.

And there was something about how Madison's elbow was touching mine on the armrest between us that made me want to know what her bedroom looked like.

I nodded.

Madison grinned and let off the brake as the light turned green, and the cars in front of us pulled forward.

"Besides," she said, making a right and pressing into the gas. "It's not even a full moon. Everyone knows you do your murdering on full moons."

She was laughing all the way down Westshore, and I gripped the seat belt across my lap, wondering what the fuck I was getting myself into.

Madison's house sat at the top of a long, steep driveway, nearly hidden from the road by evergreens and sugar maples. The house itself was massive, sprawling along the hilltop, with a three-car garage on one end and a collection of steep sloping roofs and wide windows on the other. The stone driveway formed a circle around a small fountain and a perfectly landscaped hedge, and Madison parked her car along the circle, not bothering to roll up the windows before she killed the engine and got out.

I followed, almost dutifully, as if waiting for a punchline. Waiting for Madison to toss her blond hair over one shoulder and laugh in my face—*you really thought I wanted to hang out with you?* But she didn't. She carried her bag up the front walk with me in tow, our flip-flops smacking on the stone walkway.

The huge double front door was dark wood with black fixtures. Madison pushed it open—it was unlocked.

"Fucking *Remi*." She cursed, kicking off her flip-flops beside a pair of topsiders already by the door.

"My brother," she clarified, as I slid my shoes beside hers. "He likes to show up randomly during the summer and annoy the fuck out of me. He's probably downstairs hotboxing the theater room."

There were so many insane things she'd said in a few seconds that I hardly knew what to address first. Some stoner brother? A *theater room*?

I followed Madison up one side of the staircase that flanked the huge open foyer, still shocked into silence by everything I was taking in. She moved through all of it so easily, and I tried to imagine her life as a cliché from a teen drama—the beautiful rich girl. If she lived up to the stereotype, she was hiding something. That would make two of us.

I watched Madison's hair brush the middle of her back as she walked down the hallway to a set of double doors. She grasped both handles and pushed inward, revealing a sprawling sleeping area with a low bed off to one side and a sitting area with a sofa and floor pillows facing a huge television on the other. There was even a gas fireplace built into one wall, and the far wall was taken up by French doors that led out to a small balcony. At least three of my bedrooms at home could fit inside hers.

I stood in the doorway while Madison crossed the room to her bed—it had to be a king—draped in an airy down comforter and strewn with throws and big square pillows. She shrugged out of her bathing suit coverup and fell onto the bed in her black bikini, picking up an iPad from her side table. With a few taps, music filled the room from speakers I hadn't noticed were built into the ceiling.

I immediately recognized the song. They say scent memory is strongest, but for me it was sound. And this song pulled me straight out of my body and dropped my bones into the summer before, when I was lying on a bedroom floor with my fingers wound between someone else's, a bullet shaped like a girl, and she was singing along with that song, her cheek brushing mine. We spent all summer draped over one another, listening to that album, whispering lyrics to songs about cardigans and a season that was slipping away.

"You can come in, you know."

Madison's voice pulled me back to my body, and I stepped into her bedroom, the carpet plush under my bare feet. I felt strangely underdressed in my black shorts and red lifeguarding one-piece, standing in the middle of this girl's bedroom, this girl who I only knew by name and the lounge chair she chose at the club pool.

She nodded toward the space beside her. I crossed the room and lowered myself onto the low platform, sitting cross-legged near the end of the mattress. She watched me, looking mildly amused, and I felt like prey that had willingly walked into a trap.

How had I gotten there? How had I gone from arguing with Lottie Sutherland to sitting on Madison Frank's bed in the same afternoon?

While I tried to put the events together, Madison turned to face me, folding her legs to match mine.

"Why did you invite me over?" I half blurted out the question, watching her, trying to see if her face changed.

She shrugged. "I told you. My friends are boring. The ones who were at the club? They suck. All they ever wanna do is follow around mediocre boys like little puppy dogs. That's where they went after leaving. And I saw you"—she shrugged again—"and figured I would say hi. I'm sure you're going to Willow Creek High in the fall, yeah?"

I nodded. I was staring at her incredulously, but she didn't seem to notice.

"So, you could use a friend going into that place," Madison went on. "It's a shit show."

I tried to imagine a universe where a girl like Madison would ever have issues in high school. To girls like her, high school is a kingdom to be ruled.

"What do you mean?"

Madison leaned back, pulling out her night table drawer and taking out a small box. She set the box between us and unpacked its contents—a small pipe, a nugget of weed in a prescription bottle with the label ripped off, and a lighter. I watched her pick through the weed and pack the bowl of the pipe on the top of the box while she spoke.

"There are more shitty politics at that school than at the Republican National Convention. Everyone's got something to say. And everyone thinks they're the center of the universe, but they're really only the center of their own. No one gives a fuck about anyone but themselves."

The bitterness in her voice gave her words a knife-sharp edge. Someone, or someones, at Willow Creek High had wronged her, and whatever they'd done had her ready to throw the entire school under the bus.

"Sounds like my old high school," I said, my gaze on her hands as she packed the pipe with the end of her lighter.

She shook her head.

"Nah," she said, looking up. "Willow Creek is a breed of its own."

She held the pipe to her lips and flicked on her lighter, taking a long pull. Once she let out a cloud of smoke into the space between us, she offered me the pipe. I was still trying to discern what kind of hurt the people in this town had inflicted on her, as if I might see scars underneath her skin. Her skin. So much of it bare and sun bronzed. A warmth came off her that I was close enough to feel.

I grabbed the pipe from her and took a hit. I hadn't smoked in months, not since Philly, and even then, it was always shitty weed from Carlos in Fairhill. That one pull from Madison's little glass pipe hit me quick, and I felt air collect between my brain and my skull, like an inflating balloon, pulling my head up from my shoulders.

We passed the pipe back and forth a few times until we spent the bowl, and Madison put everything on the night table so we could sprawl across the wide mattress, our chlorine summer hair fanned out on the duvet cover, our eyes fixed on the ceiling. The music had faded into a Lana Del Rey track, her soft, crooning voice floating around the space above our bodies.

Maybe it was the weed, or the warmth of Madison's arm by mine, but boldness found its way into my mouth. I looked over at her.

"Why don't you like going with your friends to hang out with guys?"

It seemed like the only missing piece of this '90s teen movie puzzle—some conventionally beautiful boy that she could tuck her body against, who she could kiss in swimming pools and who would fuck her until he left for college and forgot about her.

But Madison only chuckled beside me, her half-closed eyes still focused on the ceiling.

"You mean, why would I rather invite over a stranger than spend time with high school boys?"

"It's a fair question."

"Are you not satisfied?" she answered, playfulness in her voice as she rolled onto her elbow, resting her head on her palm, facing me. "You got a ride. I smoked you out. Do you need more? My life story?"

I felt myself smile and pulled my bottom lip between my teeth. I never could understand how girls laced their entire beings together before ever knowing anything about each other. Like some magnetic force brought us to the same space, so we could connect like broken pieces, molding to fit the other's sharp edges. How two girls could lock eyes across a crowded room and find safety in the mere knowledge of the other's existence.

I knew that power too well. Knew the consequences of letting a pair of pretty eyes pull me into the deep. But here I was, offering my hand so Madison could tie a cinder block to my wrist and push me off the dock. So ready to ruin myself for the shape of something I was sure I already knew.

"I think," I began, the drugs thick on my tongue, making the words hard to spit out. "I think I need *a lot* more."

Madison's eyes flashed with interest. I could swear I saw her lick her lips, hungry.

I felt her move closer, her breath on my face, the smell of chlorine in her hair. Every muscle in my body tensed and relaxed, a little tremor rolling through me from limb to limb. After only a few hours of learning her face, with the curve of her jaw, the shape of her eyes, and the way her lips moved, I felt like I'd already memorized her. This perfect stranger. This hallucination of a dream seeping into my waking world. Madison Frank, and the way her bikini strings had loosened since we'd laid down. My eyes followed the black strings over the gentle curve of her collarbone, down to the lift of her breasts, the valley of her chest between.

When she kissed me, I was sure I dreamt it. Her parted lips met mine, and I left my body, finding myself back on my old bedroom floor in Philly, pressed against a different body, a different girl, tasting another kiss that would tie me like a noose.

The sharp crack of thunder outside broke our mouths apart. Madison gasped.

"Fuck, I left my windows down."

We both jumped up, laughing and high, running out into the rain to her car in a haze that hung between our bodies even after the windows were rolled up and we were sprawled inside, wet and catching our breaths.

Madison laid back against the driver's seat, angling her lithe body toward me, a smile on her lips, a lock of wet blond hair stuck to her cheek.

Somehow, that boldness I'd tasted earlier found its way back into my limbs, making me lean over from the passenger seat to kiss her again, to hold her wet face between my hands and slide my fingers through her tangled hair. I'd taken a hit of something strong, and I had already forgotten how to live without it. A junkie.

I felt her lips turn up into a grin against my mouth.

We pulled back, and Madison ran her thumb over my kiss-swollen lips, studying me.

"Where did *you* come from, Tillie Gray?" She breathed the words out, and I breathed her in. I let her sink into me like fishhooks. I was her catch, begging to be reeled in.

Chapter Three

My mother was in the living room when Madison dropped me off. She wasn't supposed to be home until after 10, but her car was in the driveway when I got home. I ran through the rain to the front door, quickly ducking inside. My mom was on the couch in her work scrubs, legs tucked under her, a mug of tea balanced on the arm of the sofa.

"Oh, fancy seeing you here," she greeted me with a little laugh. "Weren't you supposed to be off work hours ago?"

I leaned back against the front door and dropped my bag, chewing my bottom lip, pretending to busy myself with tying my wet hair into a ponytail to stall for time.

"Oh uh—"

She lifted an eyebrow. I sighed.

"I was off at three. But I met a girl at the pool, and she invited me over."

I could feel the energy in the room shift, a tangible, ever present current between us, powered by my mom's anxiety over me. After Philly, I knew she'd be on high alert for the foreseeable future. I knew she'd worry about my every move, like I was a grenade with the pin pulled. She was scared I'd find another knot to tie myself into, another hole to bury myself in. Another way to smash my own heart.

"Well, that's good."

I could practically hear how difficult it was for her to say it. She was scared to push me away, so she kept letting me fuck up, figuring as long as she could break my fall, it was okay if I fell in the first place.

"Her name's Madison." I offered, throwing it out like a life raft between us. "How come you're home early?"

She smiled, took a sip of her tea, not fighting my subject change.

"I cut early. I'm taking Frankie's night shift next week, so I'll float my hours till then."

I nodded, my bottom lip between my teeth again. I was starting to shiver; my arms prickled with goosebumps the longer I stood in our air-conditioned living room with my skin still wet from the rain. I hated that my mom and I were still so tense with each other. She was my best friend, and in so many ways I'd grown up alongside her, the two of us relying only on one another. But since everything happened, she always seemed so unsteady around me, never wanting to be the reason I fell apart.

I crossed the room and sank onto the couch beside her, wrapping my arms around her body and leaning against her. My head on her shoulder, I took a deep breath and inhaled the lingering scent of the hospital mixed with the light, cool scent of her shampoo. She smelled like safety, like home.

Mom turned her head and pressed her lips to the top of mine, one arm looping around me to squeeze my body to hers. We sat that way for a moment, silently reassuring one another, our hold on each other anchoring us.

"Go get a shower before you freeze," she said softly after our moment passed. She gave my arm a rub.

I got up from the couch, bringing both of my index and middle fingers to my lips to kiss them before holding them out to her with a smile. She kissed hers and mirrored my action, and then we pressed our fingers together, something we'd done since I was little. A gesture we used to remind each other that the space between us was never too much. We were always within reach.

After I showered and changed into dry clothes, I sprawled on my unmade bed, my skin still tingling from touching Madison's. Under the soft twinkle of the string lights that hung across my ceiling, I closed my eyes, trying to focus on how being pressed against her had felt. That rush of blood in my ears, the anxious flutter in my chest as we'd run through the rain, the electric charge between our bodies as she drove me home. We hardly spoke other than me giving her directions to my house, but she kept throwing me little grins at every stop sign, the rain drumming on the windows half drowning out the soft music.

I unlocked my phone and searched for the song she'd been playing. Hayley Williams's voice filled my small bedroom from the Bluetooth speaker on my night table, a soft acoustic ballad I was already molding into the shape of Madison in my head. For me, people and places and events all had soundtracks. And once I assigned those songs, I could never untangle them in my memory. I wanted that afternoon to sound like the rush of something new and sweet. I wanted it to sound different than Philly.

The old memory was made of razorblades. It lingered under my skin, pushing to the surface no matter how hard I tried to push it down, sharp and sudden and lasting. The old memory sounded like a familiar song played in a minor key, off-putting and sharp.

The old memory was of Greer.

Greer was always shifting from girl to bullet to kitchen knife and back to girl again. Sometimes she was edgeless, sometimes her edges sliced into me, forcing me to remember them. Sometimes she was the pincushion, sometimes she was the pins. But she was always, always beautiful. No matter how much she scared me, no matter how much I wished I could forget her taste, the way her soft body felt under my hands, its gentle curves. How those curves became a current, and me just a storm-battered shoreline, weak to her erosion.

That beauty always gave way to something else, though. It gave way to the sound of harsh rain on the roof of the beach house in Stone Harbor, to Greer's screams cutting through the thunder rattling the windows.

While I laid there in bed in Willow Creek listening to the rain and the song I was trying to shape like Madison, I was thinking of the smack of my white lace-ups against the uneven cobblestones of Delancey Street, running for the SEPTA station with Greer's fingers laced between mine, both of us drinking in gulps of late October air between bursts of laughter.

There was something magical about the power we held over one another, a sweetness in the chaos of it all, like finding safety on the edge of a cliff. That, I was realizing, was the magic of teenage girls. We were all so beautiful and invincible and ready to ruin ourselves for the next thing that made us feel good.

I had never expected what Greer and I held between us to spark a wildfire. Even lying there, hundreds of miles from the ash we left behind, I could smell smoke.

My phone vibrated on the night table. I picked it up and rolled onto my side as I unlocked the screen. Madison had added her number before I'd gotten out of the BMW. She'd put a purple heart beside her name, which was now popping up in my notification bar.

tomorrow

The word chimed through by itself first, then the rest of the message followed.

i wanna show you something. i'll pick you up at 10.

I set my phone on my pillow and rolled onto my back again, my fingers touching my lips, thinking of how Madison's had felt against them.

It had only taken an afternoon for me to know that Madison could destroy me. And fuck, I wanted her to.

Chapter Four

When Madison pulled up outside my house the next morning, I was waiting inside the front door, watching out the side window. I was trying not to appear anxious, trying not to look like I'd been standing there for the last half hour. My mom had been milling around the kitchen behind me, and I could feel her gaze, but she busied herself with the dishes or absently rearranging things in the fridge whenever I looked back at her. She was hovering while trying to appear like she wasn't, a dance she'd been trying to perfect since we moved.

The BMW pulled into the driveway and even from inside the house, I could see the sun reflecting off Madison's sunglasses, see the way she'd tossed her blond hair up in a bun.

My insides backflipped.

"I'll be back later, Mom," I called behind me, pulling the

front door open—only after I'd waited a beat for Madison's text to hit my phone screen: outside.

"Hey, Til—"

"Yeah. I know. I'll call if I'm gonna be late."

"Wait a second, will you?" Mom stepped out of the kitchen, holding a dishcloth, propping her fists on her hips.

"What?"

She sighed. I waited, my hand gripping the doorknob, impatient. I knew she was trying to decide whether to set a boundary or to let me go. And I knew that she was terrified to do the former, fearful that if she acted too much like a mother, I would go down the same path I'd been on in Philly. She was worrying that Madison would be another Greer. That the only thing at the end of this road was a fiery crash.

"Nothing," she said, dropping her hands. "Be careful, okay?"

I gave her a nod and she smiled. I shrugged off the guilt that was starting to weigh down my shoulders.

I pulled the door shut behind me and jogged across the lawn, my backpack over one shoulder. I had no idea where Madison was taking me, but I knew I'd let her take me anywhere. I'd thrown on a pair of jean shorts and a dark purple tank crop top. I'd been thinking of the purple heart Madison had put next to her name in my phone. And, more than a little, I'd wanted her to notice the way my body looked in something other than my boring red one-piece from lifeguarding. I wanted her to notice the thin swath of bare skin between the hem of my top and my high-waisted shorts. I wanted her to memorize the crests and valleys of my collarbone, the way I'd memorized hers the day before.

I wanted her to notice me the way I couldn't stop noticing her.

I had my hair on top of my head in a loose bun that mirrored hers, and when she looked up to see me pulling the passenger door open, she grinned. She was wearing an almost identical outfit, but her shorts were black, and her top was a deep emerald green that tied behind her neck, leaving her shoulders bare.

She pointed to two iced coffees in the cupholders in the center console as I slid into the passenger seat and buckled in.

"I wasn't sure how you took yours, so I got you what I always get. Cold brew with oat milk and vanilla."

I picked up the drink she pointed to as mine and took a long sip. It was subtly sweet and smooth, and all I could think was how Madison's lips must taste like it too.

I was practically vibrating to be beside her again, but Madison was a basin of calm. She switched the song, and the Cardigans' "Love Fool" came on. She started to sway a bit with the music as she checked her reflection in the rearview mirror, and then looked at me again.

"Okay, you ready?"

"Where are we going?" I took another sip of the coffee, eyeing her over the cup.

Madison shrugged.

"You'll just have to trust me, won't you?"

The way her lips split into a grin made me shiver, even with the June warmth pouring through the sunroof. Madison put the car back in drive and pulled off from the curb, the wind catching the stray baby hairs that had fallen from her bun as she navigated my neighborhood at least twenty over the speed limit.

Once we'd sped through Willow Creek and gotten onto the highway outside town, Madison opened the center console and plucked out a neatly rolled joint, putting it between her lips. She steered with her knee as she covered the joint and lit it with a hot-pink Bic, taking a long pull to get it started before she offered it to me. I took it, watching Madison from behind my sunglasses while I took a hit. There was something about being with her that made me feel high before I'd even inhaled. In my head, I was molding her to fit every teenage dream I'd ever had, all while I could still feel the remnants of Greer scratching at the back of my throat. The last time I'd let myself get addicted to someone, it destroyed me. But I was still willing to do it again.

The music shuffled from the Cardigans, to Taylor Swift, to girl in red, and to Peach PRC, those sweet pop melodies swimming between us as she drove. We were mostly silent, handing the joint back and forth until she stubbed it out and tucked the last half back in the center console. I studied the road signs, looking for anything familiar. At one point, I saw the exit for the Pennsylvania Turnpike toward Philadelphia, and I took a long sip of cold brew to calm the heat in the back of my throat.

"I never take anyone here," Madison said as she took an

exit after about forty minutes of driving. There hadn't been much in the way of civilization for the last few miles, and the exit we took was only populated by a single gas station and a two-lane road that wound off into the trees. At the stop sign by the exit ramp, a rusted, faded sign read HIDDEN LAKE and directed us to the right.

It was strange—I'd never been one to sit in silence so comfortably with anyone. Normally I'd be desperate to fill the empty space, to talk over the music, to ask a thousand questions, to hear anything other than the noise inside my own head. But with Madison, I was at ease in our quiet, the space between us comfortably filled up with music and the air moving through the open sunroof and windows. I didn't ask her any questions because I didn't feel like I had to know everything. I was content, for once, to let her have the upper hand.

Madison tapped the brakes after driving another fifteen minutes from the exit, the turnoff coming so suddenly and hidden so well among the tree line that anyone who wasn't looking would miss it completely. The BMW bumped gently down the gravel road as it wound deeper into the woods. I peered through the windshield, pushing my sunglasses into my hair to see better. Eventually the trees opened up to reveal a well-kept fishing cabin and what I presumed to be Hidden Lake glittering brightly behind it.

Madison pulled the car near the front walkway and geared it into park. She hesitated before killing the engine, letting out a laugh as she rolled up the windows and closed the sunroof.

"Guess I better remember to do this, this time," she joked, before flashing me a grin and getting out of the car. I followed suit, the two of us grabbing our backpacks from the back seat and heading to the front door. Madison unlocked it with a key hanging on her key ring, pushing open the glass-paneled door.

Inside the front door opened to a living room and kitchen. Windows and sliding doors took up nearly the whole back of the cabin, providing a view of the backyard and a dock with an expensive-looking boat that was lifted under a wood covering. The furniture all looked new and modern, from the dark-gray suede sectional to the stainless-steel kitchen appliances. A huge television was mounted on the brick wall above the fireplace facing the sectional, and a rustic chandelier hung from the vaulted ceiling over the living room. A hallway off to the right of the kitchen split into two open bedroom doors, and I could see a big, neatly made bed stacked with throw pillows and dressed in a clean, puffy white duvet inside one of the rooms.

I must have looked shocked, because Madison laughed as she closed the front door behind us and stepped beside me.

"My parents got this place a few years ago, but they almost never use it. My brother sometimes throws parties here for his shitty college friends, but I'm usually the only one who comes regularly. I spend a lot of time here. Not that my parents would know."

She tossed her backpack onto the floor by the sectional and

kicked off her flip-flops, heading into the open kitchen. I tried not to let her last few words linger in the air after she walked away or acknowledge the sting in her voice as she'd said them. That was something for another day. A day when she wasn't trying to shake the frustration out of her limbs.

I lingered by the back of the sectional, my hand awkwardly resting on the couch while my toes curled against the hardwood floor, the air-conditioning bringing goosebumps over my bare skin. I watched Madison open the freezer and take out a bottle of vodka with a fancy-looking label, then pull a bottle of pink lemonade from the fridge. She plucked two glasses from the cabinet and filled them with ice, her eyes flashing to me.

"Don't tell me you don't drink." She lifted an eyebrow.

I shook my head, joining her in the kitchen. I leaned on my elbows against the center island, my eyes following her every move.

"No, I do. Just been a while." I shrugged.

Madison filled each cup about three-quarters full of pink lemonade, then opened the vodka and topped off the glasses, giving each a stir with a straw before she slid one to me. She lifted hers to me, and I grinned and lifted mine.

"What're we toasting?"

"To new friends," Madison said, and I swore I could see the fire in her eyes blazed brighter, hotter, as she said it. She clinked her glass with mine, and we both took long sips, our eyes locked over the rims of our glasses. The alcohol burned my throat; the drinks were strong, but only the sweet, tart lemonade taste lingered.

"Why'd you bring me out here?" I finally asked.

Madison studied me so intently that my cheeks flushed. I took a sip of my drink to busy myself, wincing a little as I swallowed it back. After a moment, a smile split her face. She lifted one shoulder in a shrug.

"I wanted to be alone with you."

I wasn't expecting the sudden rush of blood to my head, the room tipping under me until it felt as if my feet were on the ceiling, and I was watching me and Madison below. The last time I'd heard those words—standing on the pier outside the beach house in Stone Harbor—Greer's fingers were hooked under the waistband of my jean shorts as she tugged my body closer, the gathering storm clouds breaking open over top of us. She ignored the downpour and gripped the back of my neck when she kissed me.

By the time I tumbled back into the present, my voice was speaking without me asking it to: "Why, though?"

Madison let out a soft laugh and took a long swig of her drink.

"Can't you tell, Tillie Gray?" She set her glass down, then moved both of our drinks aside on the wide kitchen island before pulling her body up onto it, a grin brightening her face. She crawled across the island on all fours in front of me, loose strands falling free from her blond bun and framing her face, which was inches from mine now as she lowered her head toward me.

"A girl like you is the reason I don't want to follow mediocre boys around like a puppy dog."

I could smell the sweetness of her breath.

"I don't kiss just any girl in my car in the pouring rain."

This time, it was me smiling.

"Yeah well," I started, barely able to find my own voice. "I do."

My joke made her grin, and I held my breath, feeling her ease in closer until her lips were almost on mine. Instead of kissing me, she pulled back and hopped down from the island.

"C'mon, there is something I wanna show you. We gotta take the boat."

We put on our flip-flops, and I followed her to the sliding doors at the back of the house, watching her shoulder blades move under her skin and trying to shake the electricity from my bones.

Madison grabbed a key on a floating keychain hanging from the hook by the back sliding door, and we carried our drinks and the bottles of vodka and lemonade down the wide lawn toward the dock. I knew she had a joint in the crossbody she'd thrown over one shoulder, with that hot-pink Bic and the travel-sized spritzer of Coco Mademoiselle tucked beside it.

I followed Madison down the dock to the boat lift. She lowered the boat into the water, and we jumped down. I had yet to ask where exactly she was taking me. But at this point, I'd already blindly followed her enough that a mysterious boat trip couldn't have fazed me.

The lake was wide and long, curving around a bank of forest on the other shore. Madison guided the boat along that shoreline, accelerating on the other side. I watched the wind catching the stray hairs falling from her scrunchie, watched her focus behind her sunglasses as she guided the boat to the farthest bank around another curve. Finally we arrived at a wilted pier. Madison pulled the boat alongside it and directed me to jump off, so she could hand me the rope. I followed her direction, securing the rope around two cleats on the dock. Once the boat was secure and she'd killed the engine, I offered her my hand, which she gripped tightly, pulling herself up. For a moment, we were so close, her body almost against mine as she caught her balance and gained her footing. She flashed me a smile and pushed her sunglasses into her hair. I felt a hundred little fires light under my skin.

We trekked silently down the dock, and I followed Madison into the grass at the bank, heading to the tree line. I kept close, and when I fell a step behind, she threw a glance over her shoulder and held out her hand. I felt another pulse of electricity in her fingertips as she laced her fingers through mine.

"It's just up here," she said, nodding toward a break in the trees. We stumbled through a tangle of roots and branches emerging in a clearing, which I could then see was dotted with headstones. A few mausoleums jutted up from the overgrown grass, their iron doors rusted and loose on their hinges, stained-glass windows cracked and broken. In the far corner, curtained by the vines of a willow tree, was a small structure I couldn't quite make sense of.

It was shaped like a little house—a child's playhouse. Madison led me across the overgrown cemetery toward it. The shingles on the playhouse's roof were worn and breaking off, the white paint on the bricks faded and chipped. It was small, but not so small that an adult couldn't fit through the front door, which was painted a sky blue. The shutters, painted the same blue, were in disrepair, most hanging on from one hinge, with slats broken or fallen out. I was jarred with how familiar and strange it was all at once. I shivered a little despite the June heat.

The playhouse, I noticed, was part of a burial plot that was enclosed by a short, white picket fence. In what served as the side yard for the playhouse were three modest gravestones in a triangle formation. Madison stepped over the fence and bent down to brush the leaves and grass off the stones. I read each one out loud as she cleared them: "Moira Holloway...Jack Holloway...Poppy Holloway..." I squinted to see their birth and death dates. Moira and Jack died as adults, born in the early 1900s and passed away in the 1970s. But Poppy died young. Poppy was born in 1935 and died in 1944. She didn't even make it to her ninth birthday.

"Do you know what happened to her?" I wondered, as Madison continued cleaning the plot. She picked up fallen willow branches, tossing them outside the fence.

"I know a lot about Poppy," she said, not stopping her work. "I found this place when my parents bought the cabin. We took the boat around the lake, checking out the trails. I wandered off and discovered this place. And I became obsessed with finding out everything I could about Poppy Holloway. I was about thirteen at the time, and I'd just..."

She paused for a moment, kicking aside another pile of leaves. She glanced at me, then looked back at the ground.

"I had just gone through some shit, and I guess I was looking to focus my fucking brain on something else. And I found Poppy. Turns out, Poppy lived nearby on the lake. The house is still there, but the people who bought it built onto it, so it's nothing like it used to be. But she lived there with her parents. I found a bunch of news stories about them. They were pretty wealthy. Her dad was high up in the steel industry, and with the Pennsylvania Railroad. Apparently even when the Depression hit in the thirties, he hardly took a beating, which is saying a lot, 'cause I guess things *really* went to shit here.

"That was also around the time Poppy was born. She wasn't some sob story from the start. She was a regular kid. But her parents were dealing with the fallout from the Depression, laying off steelworkers, and all that shit. I guess Jack had to lay off hundreds and hundreds of them from his company. But, like I said, he still had his cushy lake house, his kid still had an au pair, and they still hosted parties for the ultra-wealthy.

"So I guess someone Holloway laid off got pissed. I mean, people were losing *everything* back then. They were homeless, they were hungry, they were dying. This guy took a dinghy out on the lake while Poppy was swimming. He fucking drowned her as some kind of retribution against Holloway. He drowned her and then he tied a cinder block to his own foot and jumped into the water."

Madison took a long pause, and I felt a breath leave me. I was hugging myself, like I was cold, despite the sweat trickling down the back of my neck. I stared at Poppy's gravestone, my eyes tracing the lines of her name and the numbers marking the viciously short time she was given. My ears were ringing, rushing with the sound of water. Waves hitting the shoreline in Stone Harbor. The sound of sobbing, muffled by the current. I felt my heart leap into my throat. I tried to stay grounded, to not slip into a panic. It had been months since I'd had a full-on panic attack, but hearing about this girl, imagining her fighting for air while hands held her under, made me grip my elbows until my knuckles turned white.

Though she was a stranger to me, a ghost story, it seemed like Poppy was family to Madison. A lost little sister. I watched Madison stop kicking around the leaves and stray branches in the plot, arms loose by her sides. She pushed the stray hairs on her hairline back, then looked at me.

"Her dad built this," she went on. "I guess he'd been planning on building her one at their house and never got around to it while she was alive. So he built this here. And I read that he and his wife kept it up. They'd come decorate it for holidays. They put her favorite toys inside, and they kept it tidy and clean. Up until they got too old to do it. And when they both died, there was no other family to do it."

The silence settled between us when she finished. I turned to examine the playhouse again. Inside the cloudy windows, I could see the outlines of dolls and other toys and a little rocking chair. I looked back to Madison and saw her looking at me. A spark ran through me again. It made me smile at her, and I let go of the protective grip I had on my torso.

"Why don't we do it?" I asked, gesturing toward the playhouse.

"Do what?"

"Fix it. Make it look nice again."

Madison looked surprised, but I saw a smile force its way onto her lips, an incredulous kind of smile, like she wasn't quite sure she believed me.

"Wait, for real? You'd wanna do that?"

I shrugged. I took in the playhouse's chipped paint and broken shutters, trying to mentally calculate whether I even knew where to begin fixing it.

"Sure, why not? Nothing a few trips to Lowe's and some YouTube tutorials couldn't handle, right?"

I had hardly known Madison for a full day, and I was already prepared to spend the rest of my summer tangling all my spare hours with hers. Throwing my body into the passenger seat of her BMW, lugging cans of paint and power tools and cases of spiked seltzer onto the boat to come out here to this secluded spot. A spot she had chosen to share with me, one she hadn't brought any of her other friends to see. Our own country, where we could claim the land and build walls around our teenage limbs, protect ourselves from the watchful eyes of the country club moms and the Westshore gossip.

Madison was smiling at me in a way I hadn't seen yet. It was bright but tinged with a sadness hidden in the corners of her eyes. As if, maybe, it wasn't often that people were kind to her without expecting something in return. I was already starting to realize who she was—a girl who could disappear from her house for days and go completely unmissed by the people who lived there. While the rest of us were clamoring for the freedom to be left alone to make our shitty choices, she wanted to be noticed in a way that mattered. I was starting to think maybe she wanted someone to look beyond the glittering grin and see the little girl who had wandered off and found this playhouse, who had mourned a drowned child she'd never met.

I had a feeling those girls she'd been sitting with at the club pool didn't know this Madison at all. I had a feeling they never would.

Madison lifted a hand to touch my face. It was cool against my cheek, which had flushed in the humid early afternoon, and only turned redder with her touch.

"Are you real?" she asked softly, studying me.

I studied her back. Her green eyes looked lighter than they had as she'd hovered over me in her bed. I wanted to learn every shade of green they could be.

"You know, I asked myself that once after I'd taken an edible, and it really sent me down a spiral," I joked, never knowing when to shut the fuck up and let someone be kind to me. Before that kindness could hurt me. Or really, before it gave me the chance to hurt someone else. I'd done too much of that. It wasn't a habit; it was a hobby.

But Madison met my match strikes with more kindling every time. She drew her hand back from my cheek and laid a soft, playful smack against it. We both grinned.

One day was all it took, and we belonged to each other in the way that only girls could.

Girl magic.

What we didn't know, yet, was if this magic was the stuff of fairy tales, or of nightmares.

Chapter Five

Greer hadn't told me that Emma was coming. When Greer's Subaru Outback pulled up outside the townhouse, Emma was sitting in the passenger seat. My seat. I saw Emma take in my house—a tiny row house that didn't even break eight hundred square feet, squished between two other identical row houses in an alley off Bainbridge. It was modest and small, but it was what my mom could afford in Bella Vista, where my school was. And I could see the judgment on Emma's smug face. She lived in Bella Vista too, but her house wasn't tucked away in an alley. Hers was a big brownstone on 8th Street, one of the newer builds that my mom and I hated because they all looked the same.

But there was Emma, sneering up at my little house—at me—from *my* seat in Greer's car, her weekend bag at her feet.

I stared at Greer through the open car window, knuckles white from gripping my backpack straps, wishing I could set the car on fire with my eyes. Let Emma Charles and her stupid fucking face go up in flames in front of me. She dared to smile at me, glossy pink lips parting to show off her stark white, straight teeth. Emma's fire-red hair fell in perfect waves against her shoulders, her big eyes hidden behind oversized sunglasses.

"Greer?"

It was all I could muster. I stared at Greer, half pleading, half hoping the rage wasn't escaping through my pores.

"Emma's parents went to New York for the weekend. She's gonna come to the beach house with us."

I knew if I turned and went back into my house, Greer would drive away. After the few weeks we'd had, I knew she wouldn't hesitate to leave me behind. There was an angry, lingering itch in the back of my mind that she'd orchestrated this to spite me, to get back at me for all the petty arguments and shitty attitudes I'd taken up with her since the start of summer.

If I was a kitchen knife, Greer was a machete. She always knew how to cut deeper.

"Whatever," I mumbled, letting my backpack drop from one shoulder.

I reached for the door handle to the back seat.

Emma leaned out of the passenger window, resting her head on her pale white arms, watching me.

"Did you know when you got in the car? Did you know what would happen?"

I felt the uneven pavement shift under my lace-ups.

The row houses turned upside down, all the front doors opening.

Dark ocean water started pouring into the alley, washing over my feet.

I stumbled back from the car, water splashing up my legs, quickly deepening. Emma smiled at me from the passenger window, water starting to wet the ends of her hair.

"Did you know what would happen, Tillie?"

———

I woke up gasping for air, swearing I could still feel the saltwater filling my lungs even though I felt my body land back in my bed. Sweat slicked down my neck. I kicked off the duvet and caught my breath, running my hands over the cool sheets to be sure I was on dry land. To be sure my bedroom wasn't about to flood with seawater.

Emma was still there in my mind, a blur of red. A faraway echo of laughter. I could hear Greer screaming, forcing a dull pain behind my eyes. No matter how many months settled between me and what happened, it felt as fresh as a new wound.

Emma wasn't supposed to come that weekend. She wasn't supposed to fucking come.

The clock on my nightstand read 3:42 a.m. My mom's night shift went till seven, and the quiet of the house felt uneasy. I got up from bed and snatched the empty glass from my night table to fill it in the kitchen, my neck still hot and damp with sweat.

Everything in the house was so still. The wood floor groaned softly under my feet. The fridge hummed as I filled my glass at the sink. Outside, I could hear the rain starting, a quiet patter on the roof. Since last summer, I hadn't been able to sit in silence very well. Silence gave my mind too much space to let the memories flood back in, the noise of it all turning up in volume.

My laptop was on the kitchen table. Before I could talk myself out of it, I sat down and opened the screen, adjusting my eyes to the blue light. I knew I shouldn't look. My mom always told me to leave it alone, to stop checking, to stop reading about it. She was terrified—of what had happened, but even more so, what it had turned me into. Or, rather, what it had revealed about who I was all along.

I opened Google, and my fingers followed muscle memory, typing *emma charles philadelphia pa* in the search bar. The first thing to appear on the results page was her school picture from sophomore year—long red hair falling in neat, loose curls against her shoulders, face forever fixed in that bright white smile. She looked young. She looked like someone's kid. She didn't look like the girl who used to comment **cute for a dumb bitch** under all my Instagram photos. She didn't look like the girl who once made it her mission to steal everything from me, to turn every friend I had against me, to poison everything good in my life.

Girl magic wasn't always used for good. Emma used hers to pillage and spoil and destroy anything in her way. And I was in her way.

I scrolled down to the first link to a news story. The headline was one I had read a thousand times, but it still made my bones ache.

Body of Missing Bella Vista High School Student Found

When I clicked the link, there was another photo of Emma, this one pulled from her Instagram account. It was of her and Greer, arms hooked around one another's shoulders, grinning into the camera with Stone Harbor's Main Street behind them.

I didn't realize I'd been biting the inside of my lip until I tasted blood. I loosened my jaw, and the tension made its way down my spine.

Emma wasn't supposed to come that weekend. She wasn't supposed to come.

I snapped the laptop closed and got up, taking my glass of water back to my bedroom.

The dark and quiet made me anxious. My pulse felt too quick. From my bed, I turned on the string lights that hung along the walls, then I picked up my phone and opened Instagram.

I tapped the top corner, toggling over to my burner account, the one I used to check on people I didn't want noticing me checking. I opened Emma's profile. I wondered why her parents hadn't had it taken down yet. Instead it stayed there with the last photo she posted, like she might post something again.

The photo was from the day it happened. Greer took it. Emma was on the rooftop deck of the Stone Harbor beach house, sitting in one of the chaise longues and wearing a red bikini. Her hair was piled on top of her head in a messy bun, eyes covered by her oversized sunglasses. She was grinning like she was in the middle of a laugh, her hand lifted halfway to her mouth, legs crisscrossed on the lounge.

I could see Greer's shadow in the photo, and a piece of another shadow beside hers.

Mine.

The photo held the ghosts of three girls who didn't know what was about to happen. Three girls who didn't realize the day would end in a night that lasted for weeks. That one of them wouldn't make it back to Philadelphia. That another would spend the weeks after in tears and grief.

And that the last would return with a secret so sharp it made her bleed every time she took a breath.

Chapter Six

"Hey—stop running on the deck, or I'll tell your mom you stole from the bar."

Gigi spoke around the whistle in her mouth. She held out the foam rescue tube to slow a little redheaded kid with sunscreen smeared thickly on his cheeks. He stared up at her with his mouth half open, then narrowed his eyes into a glare.

"I didn't steal anything!"

"Then I guess you better stop running on the deck, you overgrown Chucky doll."

Gigi let the kid pass and he huffed, speed walking away. I watched her with an amused grin, leaning on the lifeguard stand, twirling my own whistle around my fingers as she approached me.

"Stupid little monsters," she mumbled, pushing her

sunglasses onto her head once she got under the umbrella with me, rescue tube propped against her hip.

"Gi, I've always admired your passion for protecting the children," I said, giving her shoulder a nudge. "So noble. Lifeguard of the year."

"That redheaded nightmare pukes on this pool deck, without fail, at least once a week, and it's *always* on my shift," she complained. She threw another warning glance at the kid as he hurried past again, his steps slowing at her glare.

"If he'd quit running around after scarfing down like, four frozen Snickers bars, maybe I wouldn't have to mop up after him every five to seven business days."

Of all the people to share an afternoon shift with, Gigi was my favorite. She was shorter than me by an inch or two, but she could swim twice as fast, and sometimes if we closed the pool together, we'd race in the lanes in the dark before we left. She'd been one of the first people to really talk to me when I moved to Willow Creek the month before, and I found myself clinging to her the way you do with anyone who shows you the slightest attention when you're the new kid. Her parents owned a bookstore near the small state college campus the next town over, and they stocked it with everything from textbooks to Korean-language novels to used copies of old cookbooks from the sixties. There was a little coffee shop inside the store, and when Gigi had taken me there in her hand-me-down Corolla, she'd make us iced lattes with Korean banana milk and fresh whipped cream.

She'd been the one to train me when I got the lifeguarding job at the club. On my first day she handed me my whistle and said, "All you really have to do is make sure the rich kids don't drown and their bored nannies don't bring glass onto the pool deck, and you'll be fine."

Gigi never said anything to me about Madison and her friends. But sometimes I'd catch her staring at them with a faraway expression, like she had once wanted to be in their group, but now didn't dare try.

I looked over to the cabana Madison and her friends usually claimed and found a set of green eyes watching me over the top of Gucci sunglasses. Madison's friends were chatting around her, pink lips spilling laughter and words I couldn't make out. All of it went in slow motion while she looked at me. I felt, then, how Gigi must have. Outside something, but unsure what it really was, or if I wanted to be inside it at all.

"Liam said he saw you leave with the queen the other day," Gigi said, shifting the world back into focus. As if a switch flipped, the noise around me turned back on. My ears flooded with kids splashing and screaming and the buzz of the soft rock radio station over the pool speakers.

"Who?" I asked, my brain lagging.

Madison had gotten up from her lounge and crossed to the bar. Jackson was on duty, and he flashed her a grin. She looked back over her shoulder, bored. His smile fell, and he set a cup on the bar and poured her a mineral water.

"Oh. Yeah. She offered me a ride. My bike lock was stuck."

"So she randomly offered you a ride?" Gigi sounded skeptical.

I shrugged. "Yeah."

Gigi and I both watched Madison take her mineral water back to her chair, her group of friends unfolding to welcome the queen back to her hive. I was trying to place the version of Madison that I had gotten to know within the context of the version she was right now—aloof, cool. Because when she was alone with me, she was something else, entirely. Lightning in a bottle. A quick pulse and a carefully placed touch. She made me feel as though the entire universe was just scenery, and we were the supernovas on center stage.

When, I wondered, would we burn so bright we died out?

"She used to be a lot worse. And that's saying a lot."

I looked at Gigi. She glanced at me, her face flashing with guilt as she spoke about someone behind their back. It wasn't really her speed to gossip. Gigi was content to talk about the books we both read or last night's episode of *90 Day Fiancé* that we'd texted through. This was the first time I'd heard her gossip about someone else in Willow Creek, other than the occasional jab at an inattentive nanny or rude club member.

"Worse?" I pushed, still struggling to wrap that word around the image of Madison in my mind. "Worse than what? Worse how?"

"What do you mean 'worse than what'? Look at her. She and her friends were practically built to fit the popular girl group cliché. They're pretty and thin and mean. Hard to believe people like that exist outside reruns of *The O.C.*"

I peered at Madison from between the slats of the lifeguard stand's ladder. She was looking at her phone while her friends talked around her. A still life in the middle of a film reel. My phone vibrated. Glancing down, I saw Madison's name—

i spy with my little eye

Gigi went on. "I'm not trying to be the jaded nerd who hates them on principle. I've just seen what she's capable of."

something red

I looked over to Madison again. She was coyly smiling at me over her sunglasses. I nervously adjusted the straps of my red lifeguard one-piece, smiling to myself and turning away, purposely avoiding more eye contact. I could still feel her eyes behind my neck, where she'd gently pulled my hair back to press a kiss on my skin before we'd fallen asleep half drunk at the lake house.

"Yeah well," I started, clearing my throat and tightening my ponytail to busy my hands. "Everyone's capable of doing bad shit. We all have our dark side, I guess."

"Does your dark side make you call someone a gay slur in front of a full lunchroom? Or does it make you defend a guy who sexually assaulted someone?"

The lingering electricity on my skin zapped away. I pushed

my sunglasses onto the top of my head, turning to Gigi and feeling my chest tighten like someone had zipped it tight.

"I'm sorry...*what*?"

Gigi shrugged, adjusting her grip on the rescue tube.

"Her parents sent her off to a boarding school for sophomore year. Back in middle school and freshman year, she was wild. She used to get in trouble. She came back summer before junior year and something was different. She was so *mean* when she first came back. This girl at Willow Creek—well, they've come out as nonbinary now—but they were out as a lesbian during sophomore year. They dressed and looked pretty masculine, I guess, so sometimes they'd get hell from close-minded jerks at school for just, I don't know, *existing*. Anyway, they somehow crossed Madison. I don't even know what happened. It could have been next to nothing. But at lunch one day sophomore year, Madison called them a—" Gigi glanced around, leaned in closer, lowered her voice, "—a *dyke* in front of the entire lunchroom. Like, yelled it. It was so shitty. Some people actually laughed."

I felt like my insides were going to fall out of me. I tried to imagine that word leaving Madison's pretty mouth, but I couldn't hear it in her voice. I couldn't place that sharp tongue inside her mouth, a mouth I had convinced myself I knew well.

I couldn't imagine Madison being made of the same razorblades as Emma.

"Then she was dating this guy last year. Elliot James. A girl came forward and accused him of assaulting her at a party, and Madison defended him. She talked to the principal, to the cops. Swore he was with her the whole time when literally everyone knew he wasn't. But it was enough to make the girl not press charges. She left school after that. I heard she moved."

I felt like I'd been gut punched. I glanced back at Madison in time to catch her leaving the deck with her friends, disappearing beyond the gate. I was no stranger to cruel words, rude stares, and uncomfortable silences. But I couldn't overlay those things with the watercolor I'd been painting in my mind of Madison, a stark streak of thick red over the soft purples and pinks. Even after knowing Madison for only a matter of days, I felt like she wasn't capable of the kind of things Gigi was saying she did.

I swallowed back a hard gulp, feeling my throat tighten and ache.

"Sorry," Gigi said. "I probably shouldn't be gossiping about her like that. But you were bound to find out at some point, and I didn't want you to become the butt of one of her cruel jokes."

The unspoken nature of mine and Madison's new friendship suddenly felt more prickly and uncomfortable than sultry and exciting. I thought of her draped over that chaise longue under the cabana, peering at me over her sunglasses, surrounded by her pride of lionesses—all of whom had no idea she knew I was alive, much less that we'd spent multiple afternoons memorizing each other's mouths. She hadn't told me their names. I didn't have to wonder if she'd told them mine.

"I really only hung out with her that one time," I lied, too easily, some feeble attempt at soothing Gigi's discomfort. "She dropped me off at home and that was it."

She looked unconvinced, but I could tell she wouldn't push it. Gigi preferred to stay on the sidelines, where she didn't have to worry about anyone making some shitty, backhanded comment about her. At least not to her face.

"I mean, do whatever you want. I figured you should know, since you're new around here. I've seen Madison befriend new girls and then dump them later."

I knew how easy it was to shape-shift. To change yourself to suit a situation, to mirror the personalities of the people around, so they'd like you, accept you. To leave the city you grew up in and pretend nothing happened. So it shouldn't have been so difficult to imagine Madison was capable of doing the same thing. She could be what she was to me—soft, careful, a set of warm lips and a quiet voice with liquor on her breath, telling me stories about childhood summer afternoons—and then become what she needed to be for everyone else. What was hard to imagine was the version of her being so vicious. How could the Madison who mourned Poppy Holloway and cared for her forgotten playhouse be the same Madison who Gigi knew?

Gigi's whistle broke through the thick fog that swirled in my head. The redheaded kid was hurrying past us again, a frozen Snickers bar clutched in his sweaty palm.

"I said *walk*." Gigi scolded him. She pointed two fingers at her own eyes then at him, signaling that she was watching him, and he stomped off.

"Freaking kids." Gigi mumbled to herself, turning her eyes back to the pool.

But I was somewhere else. Part of me wanted to confront Madison, to ask her outright about everything Gigi said, but the other part of me wanted to pretend I'd never heard it, to go on believing Madison was the vision I'd already built up in my head.

My phone vibrated on the lifeguard stand again.

when does your shift end?

Chapter Seven

The BMW was idling in the parking lot when I finished my shift. Madison was in the driver's seat, scrolling absently on her phone, sunglasses pushed up into her hair, which was perched in a bun on top of her head. She'd changed out of her bikini and into a pair of black cotton shorts and a formfitting white tank top. I felt my stomach perform the same backflip it did whenever I laid eyes on her.

The sun was setting on the other side of the clubhouse, shadowing the parking lot. Still, slats of sunlight peeked through, illuminating Madison's face through the windshield. She tossed her phone into the center console, then looked up. A smile crossed her lips when she saw me. I felt the magnetic pull, the desperate tug of our bodies toward one another that had somehow gotten stronger. I was trying so hard to be careful, to protect myself from all that girl magic, because I knew the darkness it was capable of. I knew what I was capable of when I was in its grasp.

I'd already texted my mom and told her I was going to spend the night at Madison's. She had another night shift at the hospital, though, so I knew she couldn't argue much—if she'd told me no, I probably would have done it anyway, and she would have been none the wiser. But I was trying my best to let her trust me, to tell her things and be open about what was going on. No more hiding. And no more sneaking out of the house like in Philly when I'd disappear with Greer on school nights and not reappear for days at a time. I was so easily consumed. So happy to become a willing participant in the crimes I committed against my own mom, breaking her heart every chance I got. I was trying to do better.

But I was going to spend the night with Madison. Even if my mom told me no.

I tossed my backpack into the back seat before sliding into the passenger seat, my limbs vibrating with anticipation. That vibration threw sparks into my rib cage when Madison reached over to touch me, wrapping her hand around my wrist and giving it a squeeze, her midnight blue fingernails digging lightly into my skin.

Without acknowledging the touch, Madison released me and put the car in drive.

"Turn on some music, yeah?"

Up until that point, Madison had chosen the music we listened to together, and I felt a rush of anxiety to pick the perfect soundtrack. Every memory I had was attached to a sound. It was how I revisited those feelings later. I wanted this moment to be as perfect as those we'd already had. I pulled my phone from my pocket and connected to the car's Bluetooth, scrolling through my library for the perfect song.

I landed on "Nothing's Gonna Hurt You Baby" by Cigarettes After Sex, and Madison turned up the volume, letting the smooth, soft sounds fill the car. She opened the sunroof and pulled out of the parking lot, and as we headed out of Willow Creek and toward the highway, she reached her hand over, slipping her fingers between mine, her thumb tracing soft circles against my skin.

On the drive to the lake house, everything Gigi had told me sat somewhere in the back of my mind. Not totally forgotten but pushed back far enough that I could enjoy those forty or so minutes with Madison and our music with nothing between us but the push of the night air through the sunroof. As we hit the exit for the lake house, the sun was gone from the sky and Madison's headlights cut through the blue darkness of the road that led to the turnoff.

The cabin's front lights were on, like it was waiting for us. Madison parked, and we got out, both carrying our backpacks inside. The crickets and katydids were singing loudly.

Once inside, we kicked off our flip-flops and tossed our backpacks aside, and I noticed the small collection of Lowe's bags in the foyer. A few buckets of paint, a container with some tools, and an assortment of building supplies. I nodded toward the pile.

"Is that—"

"For the playhouse," Madison finished for me, smiling. "My dad came by earlier, and I asked if he'd drop some stuff off. I guess that's what he got."

There was a warmth in my chest that brightened every time Madison said or did something particularly endearing. Since I'd suggested we restore the playhouse, she'd been buzzing over the idea. She'd even texted me pictures of paint swatches and links to YouTube videos on how to fix shutters. The things Gigi told me prickled sharply under the surface of my thoughts, but I still couldn't fit them around this Madison—the Madison who was teaching herself to repair shutters or matching the sky-blue paint on a dead little girl's graveside playhouse.

I followed her farther into the house. She kept the lights off, with only a dim light coming from a lamp in the front entrance. We settled onto the oversized sectional. Part of me wanted to resist the lunar pull of her body on mine, like my limbs were the tide. Part of me wanted to keep air between our bodies so I could see her as less of a celestial being and more of a human, someone with flaws and headaches and bad days.

But there in the low light and quiet of the lake house, in the safety of the space between us and everything we were hiding from, I couldn't help but sink into her. I let her pull me in. I let her run her hands up my arms and trace her fingertips along the collar of my T-shirt, her eyes flashing up to mine. I wondered what she was thinking, what she was trying to decipher.

My bare legs touched Madison's, tangling loosely with them as she moved in closer. She wound an arm around my neck, her fingers twisting gently into my ponytail, and I wished she'd speak. I couldn't read her, and that terrified me.

"You scare me." I heard myself breathe into the space between us, which was quickly narrowing.

Madison brushed her nose against mine. She dropped her hand to my T-shirt sleeve, her fingertips slipping under the hem.

"If you're not scared, then it isn't worth it."

She moved in to kiss me, but I leaned back, wetting my lips, my hand gentle on her collarbone, making her look at me.

"Are you scared, then?"

I tried to imagine her scared. This force of nature who carried herself so fearlessly, the girl who took me home and kissed me in the rain, though she had no idea about the darkness I'd left behind in Philadelphia. But she had darkness of her own. She had a closet full of skeletons and dark water and memories she probably wished to forget. But right here, on this couch in the lake house, we could both shed those versions of ourselves. We could lock the door and pretend there weren't monsters with mouths full of teeth waiting outside for us.

"Oh Til," Madison breathed. She touched my cheek. "I'm terrified."

It felt like a confession. A candlewick lit inside me. I leaned my body into hers, my mouth crashing into hers in an eager, almost desperate, kiss. I wasn't entirely sure what I was so desperate for—to know her? to have her?—but it consumed me. My hand moved behind her neck to keep her in that kiss, although she gave no sign she intended to pull away. Madison slid her hand down my side and under the hem of my T-shirt, her fingertips soft on my skin. Instead of recoiling in nervousness, I let her press her palm into the warm skin at the small of my back. I felt her breaths mix with mine, tasted the lingering Chapstick on her lips, the soft sweetness of her tongue when it touched mine. Madison was nothing if not assertive, hungry. But in that moment, she didn't rush us. She held on to me and let the kiss break gently.

After a beat and a breath, Madison spoke.

"I'm sorry about your friend back in Philadelphia."

I felt my stomach drop. I drew back, studying her in the low light, trying to decide if I'd heard her say what I thought I had. My head felt full of static.

"What…what friend? Who are you talking about?"

Madison gave a small shrug, her hands moving to cover mine.

"I was…scrolling back through old posts on your Instagram. I was curious about, you know, your life before you came here. I saw a picture of that girl, the one who—the one who died last year. I didn't know she was your friend. I remember hearing about it when it happened."

I could feel my chest collapsing. I'd spent months planning how I was going to avoid anyone in Willow Creek ever finding out I knew Emma Charles—I'd deleted every trace of her from my social media, like she'd never even existed to me. I shook my head, a hand going to my forehead. The room felt like it was starting to spin. Madison's face was shadowed in concern, and she reached for both my hands again, holding them in her lap.

"What? What is it? I'm sorry. Shitty timing, I shouldn't have said anything. I didn't want to know about it but not *tell* you I knew about it. You know?"

"How?" I managed to croak.

"How what?"

"How did you know I knew her? I don't have any pictures with her on my account."

Madison's cheeks reddened. She chewed her bottom lip, clearly trying to think of what to say, or how to word the truth.

"Well…I went down a bit of a rabbit hole. I scrolled through your pictures, and I saw this one girl tagged in a bunch of them. Greer something? So then I looked at her pictures. And I saw that girl Emma in a bunch of *her* pictures, and some of the posts had you in them too."

Fuck. Of course. Greer.

"I'm sorry, Tillie. Fuck, that was dumb of me to say, and right then of all times to say it—"

"I knew her," I stammered, and Madison hushed, waiting for me to go on, her eyes expectant. I tried to decide what I really knew about this hurricane disguised as a girl, and whether I should give in to the urge that was building inside me to tell her everything. Like that couch was my confessional and Madison's open palms were my altar, waiting to accept whatever sins I spilled into them—and there were so, *so* many sins to spill.

But I bit my tongue. I could taste saltwater in the back of my throat. The faint echo of Emma's laughter bounced inside my head as I shut my eyes, wishing it away. Madison gave my hands a hard squeeze. I tried to use her grip as a buoy.

Instead of spilling my sins, I turned the focus to Madison's. The spotlight on me was too bright and accusing.

"Gigi told me about Elliot James."

It was Madison's turn to recoil. She curled her fingers into tight, anxious fists in her lap.

"Gigi doesn't know shit about Elliot James."

The words came out harsh and quick, their sharp ends pointed at me. I sat still. Her face was splashed over with an emotion between sadness and fury. I couldn't tell if she was about to defend Elliot James or wish Elliot James dead in a ditch. Maybe both.

"Will you tell me what she doesn't know?"

I spoke softly, surprised at how easily I'd calmed after Emma was brought up. How easily I'd turned the conversation to Madison. She seemed to soften at my question, and I felt her body relax enough that her bent knees touched mine again. Her eyes fell, and I gave her the silence she needed to gather herself.

"It's so much more complicated than people understood. All people knew, all they saw, was me going to bat for some fucking prick who was being accused of assaulting this girl at a party. So much fucking other shit was going on that people didn't know—that they'll never know. Including fucking Gigi."

I pressed my lips together. Part of me wanted to gently encourage her to keep talking. But I let the silence sit between us, filled only by the soft hum of the fridge in the kitchen and the steady pulse of katydids outside.

"He was going to out me."

There was a familiar ache whenever someone said something like that. The struggle of realizing who we are—and then having to live with it—is one I would not soon forget. It was a complicated beauty and ache. I wet my lips. They still felt kiss swollen. I felt like I had to hold my breath.

"We were dating for a handful of months. I came back from boarding school—that's a whole fucking other story—and I just... I needed something to hold on to. Maybe something to hide behind. Elliot became that for me. He was an asshole. He was mean. Called me names, called me fat. Slut-shamed me for any other person I'd ever dated. Treated everyone who wasn't in his friend group like total trash. An all-around shit. But he was *that* guy. The one all the girls wanted, for whatever reason. For me, he was a hiding place."

I stayed still, letting her speak and trying not to interrupt her. When she waited a beat, I reached for her hand. She let me take it and curled her fingers around mine.

"He found out when I left my phone unlocked, and he looked through it. Read texts between me and a girl I used to have a thing with and who I was still talking to. He held that shit over my head—my story to tell when I wanted to, if I wanted to. Used it as leverage for everything he wanted from me. Sex. Alibis when he'd sneak out. And, ultimately, an alibi for when he was at that party. When he assaulted that girl."

There was something like anger starting to rise in my chest. That cold fire I actively tried to avoid ever since Stone Harbor. Ever since Philly. It consumed me too easily—made me someone I didn't recognize. But my insatiable need for Madison was making me angry over this faceless boy, who I'd never even seen but who I already wanted to destroy in ways too dark to name. Who was this guy to do what he'd done and go on living normally? Did he carry the same scars as Madison, the ones she was baring to me—the same ones on the girl he hurt? Did he carry any guilt at all?

I tried to stifle my anger with my confusion.

"So does that mean…" I shook my head. "Does that mean you're not out at all? To anyone? Not even your friends?"

Madison let out a laugh, shaking her head. She sniffled and swallowed. That made the cold flame of anger flare. I wanted to hurt the ones who hurt her.

"I get that people our age are supposed to be more *woke* or whatever, but the kids around here will use anything they can use as ammunition against you. Anything they can shoot at you with, anything to weigh your shoulders. Being even a little bit outside the mainstream is reason for being shit on."

Her words triggered another memory of what Gigi had told me, and I bristled, eyes narrowing.

"But…didn't you…"

Madison looked at me, waiting, and my pulse picked up.

"Didn't you...make fun of someone for the same reason?"

Shame darkened her features. Her eyes filled with tears like I'd sucker punched her. As much as I wanted to protect her, I wanted her to answer for it. I wanted to know who I was protecting.

"I was scared, Tillie. I was trying to be someone I wasn't. And I said and did disgusting things. I regret every fucking thing I did during that time. I didn't know who I was. Who that girl was. And look, I'm not perfect now. I'm still a wreck. I'm still trying to figure my shit out. I still pretend to be a version of myself that I think will make life easier. But doesn't everyone? Tell me that. Who *isn't* doing whatever they can to exist peacefully?"

I thought of the year before, how many days I'd spent watching Emma soak up Greer's attention and affection, hating every second but tolerating it, if only to stay around Greer. To be near the person I wanted to be near. I did exactly what Madison had: I created a version of myself I didn't like or recognize, just to be palatable to someone else. Besides, calling someone a slur was hardly a shadow of a sin compared to what I'd done when I'd finally snapped.

"Besides," she choked out. "It wasn't just about outing me. There was other shit Elliot had on me that could have brought my entire life crashing down if he told anyone."

As much as I'd suspected that the fear of being outed wasn't all that had driven Madison to Elliot's defense, having it confirmed felt somewhere between terrifying and relieving. Terrifying in the unknown of those secrets. Relieving to sit beside her as a twin flame, burning with the threat of potential ruin.

I dug my fingers into my palms, fists tightening until my knuckles went white. Madison covered my hands with hers, and I loosened my grip on my own body. She sat there in front of me, scars bared and fresh, secrets spilled. The urge to spill my own was visceral and deep. It pulled me toward Madison like how the water had pulled at my ankles on the beach in Stone Harbor last summer. A siren song spun from pain and longing and the relentless weight of that night feeling like cinder blocks tied to my limbs.

"I was there when Emma Charles died."

I could see Madison trying to piece the puzzle together in her mind.

"What do you mean you were there when she died?" Her words were soft and slow.

My heartbeat was thick in my ears. I watched Madison, hoping she'd understand without me having to say the words out loud.

"I thought…I thought Emma Charles went missing and was *found* dead."

It was like I could hear the blood coursing through my veins. All other noises had faded into nothing—the pulse of katydids and the hum of the fridge, all silent now. But I could hear Madison's breath, the sudden pull of air through her parted lips as the pieces fell into place.

Her eyes widened. "You know what happened?"

I swallowed the fire in my throat. My voice refused to let me explain. Instead I stared at Madison, feeling the muscle in my jaw twitch as I clenched my teeth. A tremble rolled through my entire body.

She didn't get up. She didn't point her finger at me, call me a liar, or tell me I was horrible for not telling anyone what I knew. For letting Emma's family suffer for weeks before her body was found. Madison didn't even let go of me. She squeezed my hands, her eyes fixed on me. I could practically feel the nervous, overwhelmed, excited energy vibrating off her.

We shared secrets now. All that dark magic that had wrapped itself around us now bound us together. It could only be broken if one of us wanted to destroy the other. It was terrifying. Even if Madison didn't know exactly what had happened on that night with Emma—how Emma had held on to my arms and how I'd hid the scratches, the icy pull of the ocean, the sharp stab of Greer's screams—she still knew I'd lied to the police. She knew that whatever happened to Emma Charles was different from what she'd heard on the news, and that I was one of the only people who knew the truth. One of the only ones left alive, at least.

It was ammunition enough to ruin me. And I could ruin her right back if I ever revealed how she'd covered for Elliot James. If I revealed who she really was. We'd both poured gasoline over our own lives, and we'd handed the other a match. All we'd have to do is strike and throw.

But instead of scaring us into a trembling heap, it seemed to make us a new kind of hungry, a new kind of desperate for one another. I hadn't known that kind of need since my first few months with Greer, but this was wilder, more furious.

Madison's mouth collided with mine, sending us crashing back down to Earth. I felt her body pushing mine, my hands searching for her skin as our kiss deepened. I was glad I'd changed out of my swimsuit before leaving the pool—it made it easy for Madison to slip her fingers under the waistband of my cotton shorts as she pushed me onto my back on the sofa, dragging my shorts down from my hips. I felt goosebumps rush over my exposed skin as her fingertips brushed the front of my underwear, daring to touch me in a way I hadn't been touched since Greer. My body never belonged to anyone else the way it had to her. Madison sat up long enough to pull her white tank top over her head. She was naked underneath, and I felt my lungs seize at the sight of her bare chest. My hands instinctively lifted to touch her, fingertips tracing the curves of her breasts and running back down her sides as she reached for my shirt. My pulse was racing. I was convinced she could hear my heart drumming through the quiet of the house.

I leaned up to take my shirt off, dropping it on the floor beside Madison's. We were laid doubly bare, then—our secrets, our bodies, given to each other like gifts. As she laid her torso back down to mine, her chest pressed against mine, our skin coming together, pushing the air from my lungs. My lips parted in a soft sigh as Madison's mapped the curve of my jaw. I felt her hand move between our bodies, fingertips brushing the top of my underwear before slipping beneath the fabric. I melted into her touch. My back arched from the couch as her fingers found me. I gasped and matched her, my hand snaking around her arm to slip into her cotton shorts, electricity pulsing through me as we found each other, bodies and breath. She touched me like she'd known my body in a previous life. I felt her shake above me, and I knew I was giving it right back. I wanted her to feel what I felt, to keep the electric circuit of our bodies closed until the power overwhelmed us and threw the fuse.

With my knees bent at her hips and our bodies locked together like they were made to fit, I memorized the way she sounded when she fell over the edge, committed her breaths to memory, wished I could etch her into vinyl and play her again and again and again.

I fell with her, gasping when I heard my voice form her name, felt heat on my neck and that deep warmth in the center of me. We were reduced to shivers and quick breaths.

Once we'd found gravity again, Madison brushed her lips against mine as she looked over my face, lifting her hand to push my hair back from my forehead.

"You're the most beautiful secret I've ever kept."

I knew even as she whispered those words that all I wanted was to be kept by her.

Even if it meant my ruin.

———

Before we could disappear to the lake house for the days I had off from the club, we had to make appearances at our respective homes. Mom was in and out, picking up shifts, filling her time, and I wondered if she was trying to keep herself busy to resist the urge to hover. Once she told me how when I was a baby, she would creep into my nursery while I slept and peek through the bars of my crib to watch my chest rise and fall. I thought of how she did that now, the quiet peeks into my bedroom, the gentle hovering in doorways and behind me at the kitchen table while I scribbled through homework. That ever-present, but never too-heavy, weight of her nearby.

Even after spending a few nights in Willow Creek, Madison and I couldn't stand being out of each other's orbit for too long. I'd been home a matter of eight hours before I was gathering up my things to go to her house. My mom appeared in my bedroom door, her hands full with a stack of clean laundry.

"Where are you running off to?" she asked, stepping up to set the clothes down on my bed beside my backpack. I tossed my phone charger into my bag, giving it a little shake within her line of sight before I did. She was always anxious about dead phones and unreturned messages. It took her back to the darkest days of Philly, when I'd disappear into the city, untethered.

She wrinkled her nose at my gesture, but I knew she'd needed it.

"Just to Madison's for a little while."

"Overnight?" She punctuated her question with a hesitant beat of silence. "I'm not working tonight. I was thinking we could order some Chinese, watch that movie we've been wanting to see?"

I zipped my backpack closed, tossing one strap onto my shoulder. My mom was looking at me, hopeful. I pulled in a deep sigh, thick with drama, and she reached over to pinch my side, doubling me over in a laugh as I swept out of her reach.

"Yeah, that sounds good, Mom. I'm not gonna stay overnight. I'll be home in a couple hours."

There were days I remembered how much we needed each other. And there, with her gaze on me, stack of freshly folded summer clothes on my bed, I remembered.

She hooked an arm around my neck, drawing me into her. She pressed her lips into my hair, and I leaned into her, letting both arms circle her waist. I pulled a little tighter, giving her a squeeze. We were, both of us, still learning to be the versions of ourselves that the other needed. Even there, seventeen with my arms around her, I was still that small body tucked into her zip-up hoodie.

"Be good, yeah?"

Her words were less of a demand than a wish. I nodded against her shoulder, though I wasn't sure what I was really promising with it.

Madison and I were draped across her made bed, taking turns picking songs to play over the speakers in her room. We were speaking in song lyrics that told the stories of how we felt better than we could. Even without speaking ourselves, we were saying enough. I passed the iPad back to her to let her

choose the next song, and she scrolled through her saved favor-
ites. I noticed, watching the screen, that she'd made an entire
playlist of the music we shared, titled only with three purple
heart emojis across the top of the list. While she scrolled, I saw
all the songs we listened to in her car, music we'd sent each
other over text, and the songs we played while we worked on
the playhouse. Now, as each song ended, she was adding it to
the list. A curated soundtrack of Us.

She landed on a Labrinth song, all soft vocals with sudden,
deep, dramatic drops. I watched her add the song to our ever-
growing playlist before she tossed the iPad onto her pillow
and turned over onto her side to face me. She tugged a throw
pillow under her head and tucked one hand under her cheek,
the other reaching out to play idly with the strings on my
hoodie. My thoughts floated along the current of the music
she'd chosen, but eventually picking a bit of shore to wash
up on. A thought I'd been carrying since Madison had first
mentioned being sent away to school.

"Hey, why'd your parents send you to that school?" I asked,
my voice barely rising above the crescendo of the song's bridge.

Madison grabbed the iPad from behind her and turned the
volume down, just a little.

"I was getting in trouble," she started, easily, without too
much thought or hesitation. "In middle school and freshman
year, I snuck out all the time. I hung out with older kids, so I
was like…thirteen, but running with juniors and seniors. Not
sure why they wanted me around, really. But I got caught up

in it. My parents eventually got sick of my shit and sent me to Walden. They'd been threatening it for months at that point, but I never thought they'd actually do it."

"What was it like, there?" I probed, gently. A buffer for my real question, but I wanted to build up to that.

She shrugged.

"Just a bunch of rich kids at a bougie school in upstate New York. Most of us were, you know. *Troubled.*" She chuckled at that. "Sent there as a punishment. Or really, to get us out of our parents' hair. Let us be someone else's problem."

I imagined moss-covered stone buildings lined with trees. Plaid skirts and untucked button-ups, loose ties. Black penny loafers and knee-high socks. Groups of pretty girls with long hair gathered around lunch tables like a murder of crows.

A specific pretty girl. One who had held Madison's attention and affection in the time she spent there. She had become an amalgamation of different lovely pieces in my mind since Madison had mentioned her. A collage of every pretty girl I'd ever met, wandering through the ivy-draped buildings I was imagining Walden to have been.

"You mentioned a girl," I said, starting to dance at the edges of what I really wanted to know.

Madison's light smile faltered. The corners of her lips fell, and I saw her stitch her brows together for a moment. She nodded, though, before I could panic.

"Yeah. There was a girl. Well, a few girls. I had a little group of friends I spent most of my time with, and they were my whole life while I was there. Hunter was…" She took a breath. "She was the one I got involved with. The one whose name and messages Elliot saw on my phone once I was back home, and she and I were still hashing out bullshit from when I'd been at Walden with her. We all used to sneak outta the dorm together most nights and run out to this little spot in the woods by the lake, get high and talk shit."

I imagined Hunter as that mosaic of a pretty girl in my mind. I saw, for a moment, that girl wound up with Madison in a twin bed in a dorm room. I lost the rhythm of my breath.

"And then there was…" She started again but stopped just as quickly. I waited, my mind still swimming.

"There was another girl. A girl who hung out with us sometimes. She lived in the room across the hall. She used to come with us to our spot too. We quit talking a little before I left Walden. So once I left, I really only still talked to Hunter."

This girl, unlike Hunter, was a ghost in my mind. Still without a name, she stood as a shadow in the picture I was painting. There was something in the way Madison's voice grew quieter talking about this girl and how her words came out slower, more carefully chosen, that only deepened my thirst to know her.

"What made you stop talking?"

I kept my question open, kept its edges soft. I didn't want her to pull back. Still, Madison visibly bristled. She shifted, sat up, restlessness rattling through her all of a sudden. I sat up with her, slowly, making a conscious effort not to stare at her face.

"She ran away. From school." She paused, and I noticed her stop her next sentence, holding it in her mouth. She pressed her lips together, thinking.

"It happened there a lot. People would be missing from class one Monday morning, and we'd find out later that they ran away, got kicked out, went home, or got suspended. Whatever it may have been."

It happened there a lot. I turned the words over in my mind, trying to imagine normalcy in disappearance. Trying to imagine what *whatever it may have been* could have meant.

"Never spoke to her after that. And I left Walden not long after she ran away, anyway."

I could tell Madison was trying to tie up the loose threads of this half-story so I would stop probing. So I stopped—at least right then. At least out loud.

I couldn't ask too much more, anyway, as a sudden echo of laughter from downstairs breached the quiet of the closed bedroom door. Both of us looked toward the sound. When we'd gotten to Madison's house, it had been empty. Now, a voice trailed up from the open front foyer, mingled with the sound of the front door closing, and keys being tossed.

"Fucking Remi," Madison groaned. Her brother. I remembered the edge to her voice whenever she'd mentioned him. Even without a sibling of my own, I could tell it was more than a standard-issue sibling rivalry. Madison stiffened at his voice from downstairs, and I saw her jaw set. But it was another voice—a lower one, its timbre carrying even stronger—that made her pause. She leaned in, listening harder as Remi's and the other voice drifted farther into the house. Her gaze flashed to me, darkened with confusion, and she got up, crossing quickly to the door. I followed as if by a magnetic pull, tiptoeing across the carpet. Madison carefully unlatched the door handle, easing it open a quietly as she could. As we stepped out of her room together, she turned to me and pressed her finger to her lips. I gave her a nod, curiosity already biting at the backs of my heels as we moved down the hall toward the open foyer. The upstairs of Madison's house opened down to the first floor, with a railing overlooking the foyer and stairs on one side, and the living room on the other. As we stepped closer to where the hallway gave way to the railing, Madison sank down to the floor, and I mirrored, the both of us slinking to peek into the living room below.

Two boys had dropped onto the big sectional couch and picked up video game controllers from the oak coffee table. One of them I clocked as Remi—he had the same honey-blond hair as Madison, and the same lift in his cheekbones. The other was taller, with broader shoulders, and a carefully tousled mess of dark brown hair that he pushed back with one hand.

"I'm fucking serious, bro," he was saying. "The entire school's numbers and emails are on that list, and we've fuckin' got it. You can pick any girl you want off that list and put her phone number into one of those social media search engines and find every fuckin' account she has."

"So what, though?" Remi countered. "So you get their usernames and shit. What good's that do?"

"All I'm saying is," the other boy went on. "You can find out pretty easily which of these girls has pictures that they don't think anyone can find."

Remi's face split into a grin. I felt my stomach turn.

"But if you don't wanna put in the legwork, we've already got a fuck ton of 'em. Zipped in a private cloud account. Only the dudes on the swim team have the login. Fully encrypted, end-to-end. No trace of anyone who accesses it. But if you want in, I'd practice some caution. You might see some shit you don't wanna."

I felt Madison's arm tense beside me. The muscle in her jaw twitched. The other boy was talking about photos of her.

"Aw, sick, man," Remi groaned. "No I don't wanna fucking see that shit. Just send me the good ones and weed out the rest."

Before I could properly react, Madison was getting to her feet. I followed her back to her room, my steps still light and quiet. She pushed the door shut behind us, latching it softly, and leaning her body against it.

"Who is that?" I asked, keeping my voice low.

Madison's chest rose and fell with a deep breath. Traces of anger still sat in her features.

"That is my brother. And Elliot."

"Wait, your brother is *friends* with Elliot?"

"They've always been pretty fucking chummy. But now I think Remi brings him around to piss me off."

Downstairs, laughter erupted, then shouts over whatever video game they were playing. I watched Madison close her eyes and grip the door handle. She was practically vibrating with anxious energy. I reached for her hand, gently pried her fingers from the door handle and gripped them with mine.

Every peek I got behind the curtain of Madison's life only threw gasoline on an already thirsty and curious fire. I wondered, kissing her fingertips, if she was doing it on purpose. A clever way to entice and enthrall me, to keep me hooked. But what would happen when I learned too much? When the illusion of her was no longer smoke and mirrors, but concrete and metal.

I didn't care. I would take the fallout as eagerly as I was taking the lead-up.

At home later, Mom fell asleep on the couch while we watched the movie she wanted to see. She was laid against the other end of the sofa with her legs stretched out, resting against my curled legs—a wordless way she kept tabs on me.

But even before she'd fallen asleep, I'd hardly been able to focus on the movie. All I could think about was the girl from Madison's boarding school and how carefully Madison had spoken about her. The purposeful way she avoided speaking the girl's name.

Once Mom's breathing had evened and slowed, I picked my phone up from the coffee table. I was trying to be present for her, whether out of a real desire to be better or as a means of keeping her placated, I wasn't sure. But setting my phone facedown amid half-eaten Chinese food containers when we started the movie had felt like one way to do that.

I opened Instagram and toggled to my private account. It had no followers or posts, and the username was a collection of random letters. I'd made it when Emma had first set her sights on Greer and used it as a private way to check in on her. Now, I used it to look into people in Willow Creek.

I started with Madison's profile. I tapped on her list of followers and searched for Hunter. An account popped up before I'd even finished typing. Username **hunterrrr** was exactly how I'd pictured her—a mosaic of pretty girl pieces, a sweeping length of golden-brown hair and a bright grin. When I opened her profile, which was mercifully public, I could see she was still at Walden. Her most recent photo was from two days before. She'd posted a picture of her posing in a plaid skirt and an untucked white polo shirt outside a stone building with the caption **summer school is for the birds**. It had hundreds of likes and comments, but I only noticed Madison's.

I scrolled through Hunter's posts—a perfectly curated and aesthetically pleasing grid that oscillated between what I guessed was Walden's campus and her home: a neat, suburban town she geotagged as—and I couldn't help but lift an eyebrow at—Madison, Connecticut. Her parents had a palatial house on the coast, with Long Island Sound draped behind it.

I kept scrolling, farther and farther down until I'd reached more than a year before, working backward from the time Madison left Walden to when she started there. Once I hit that row in Hunter's grid, it didn't take long to find a photo of Madison. It was from April of her sophomore year, right at the end of her time at boarding school. She was perched on a picnic table, legs folded under her, and Hunter by her side, their heads leaned in, temples touching. Behind them, the sun was setting across the expanse of a lake. The caption was a play on that line from the Frost poem: **two (girls) diverged in a yellow wood.** I wondered if that post had been a kind of goodbye.

I scrolled farther, trying to get a glimpse of who the third girl in their circle could have been. It was at least another few months back before one emerged—a snapshot of Hunter; Madison; and another pretty, dark-haired girl. I thought I recognized the girl from a photo I'd seen somewhere on Madison's profile during one late-night scroll or another. When I tapped this photo of Hunter's, the girl was tagged: **comingupdaisy.** I tapped on her tag.

Daisy.

Her profile was locked and private.

I quickly tapped back over to Madison's profile and scrolled down, searching for where I'd seen Daisy's face before. Sure enough, about a year back I found the first photo. It was Daisy, grinning with Madison, the two sitting on a set of stone steps wearing matching school uniforms. The caption read: **will be missing this smile forever. my heart is in pieces. love you always.**

My throat tightened. Heat pooled in my chest. I remembered Madison's words earlier that afternoon: *She ran away from school.... I never spoke to her after that.* The emerging answer to why they'd never spoken again was like a Polaroid developing the more I shook it.

I scrolled farther, digging deeper into Madison's year at Walden. Daisy didn't appear again until a few months earlier, a photo of the two of them on a twin bed in a dorm room, Madison's arm hooked around Daisy's shoulders, Daisy's dark hair gathered into a bun on top of her head. The two were suspended in a laugh. The caption read: **never hitting that sophomore slump with this one.**

Daisy wasn't tagged in either photo. Madison had turned off the comments on both—the only two photos in her entire grid with them disabled. I scrolled and scrolled, hitting the end of Madison's Instagram feed. Daisy never made another appearance.

I opened my browser, almost involuntarily. As I began to type in the search bar—*daisy walden school new york*—I stopped. My fingers hovered over my phone screen, staring at the search button. If I looked, if I dove into what Madison hadn't yet told me and dug her skeletons forcibly out of the hard ground, I might find bones I didn't want to see. Memories buried for a reason like a cursed rabbit's foot, all delicate magic until it turns. Until you know too much for the beauty to stay.

I tapped out of my browser. Set my phone on the coffee table again.

Some secrets were better left buried.

Chapter Eight

I spent the next three days with Madison at the lake house, sleeping in late and passing the afternoons at the cemetery, working on the playhouse. We worked together easily, our moves almost choreographed as we repaired broken shutters and primed and painted them. Madison played music on a Bluetooth speaker while we worked on opposite sides of the playhouse, one of us painting and the other cleaning the brick and scrubbing off the mold and moss with bleach and water. We went back to the lake house, sweat on our necks and hair in messy ponytails, as the sun disappeared behind the trees, the water dark and the lights on the house guiding us back to the dock. We spent the nights in one of the bedrooms, memorizing every inch of each other's bodies, whispering stories and quiet, half-awake musings as we fell asleep in the early morning hours.

I never asked her any more about Walden. Or Daisy. I let them both lie, let them stay anchored in Madison's past, an ocean I knew I'd never explore every part of.

I answered calls and texts from my mom vaguely, rushing her off the phone and promising I was fine. I knew if I didn't answer at all, she'd spiral, and she deserved better than that. I did it for so long with Greer, disappearing and reappearing only to gaslight her and call her crazy. I was fine; she was overreacting; I hadn't disappeared. At least if I answered my phone, if I played our game, she might not insist I come home. I would have done anything to stay there with Madison, cultivating the little universe we were building, safe from everyone and everything else.

On the fourth morning, we had to go back. Madison's mom had texted to tell her the landscapers were due at the lake house that day, and my streak of days off was ending. I had to be at the club by noon.

We packed the BMW sullenly, like we were dismantling our little world, putting it away to keep it safe until we could come back. As we pulled away from the house and down the long gravel driveway, I turned to look out the back window, watching our perfect weekend be swallowed by the trees that hung over the drive.

Madison turned on a playlist we had claimed as ours—a mesh of girl in red, Pale Waves, Hayley Kiyoko, and Bon Iver, and the acoustic version of that Taylor Swift song she loved so much. She stopped just off the interstate to grab us both iced coffees, and I let her order for me again, wanting to share another piece of her.

My mom would tell me I was getting lost. Again. If she knew how deeply I'd gotten in over my head already with Madison, she'd tell me I needed to take a step back and remember myself. But I didn't want to.

Madison pulled between two parked cars in the club's lot, hiding us from view so she could lean over the center console, take my face in her hands, and kiss me long and hard. It felt like a promise. A promise we'd both already made and broken to other people, but a promise all the same.

"Do you have to stay at home tonight?" she asked as I gathered my backpack from the back seat. I stood outside the open passenger door, gripping the straps.

"Probably." I sighed. "I think three days is likely my max for sleeping away from home right now. I don't wanna push it with my mom and end up on lockdown."

The clock on the dash read 11:58. I needed to get inside, but my feet were cemented beside her car.

"Can I..." she started, then stopped, chewing her bottom lip in thought. "Can I like, come stay with you? At your house? Maybe?"

The nervousness in her question felt like an anxious fist around my heart—she was as hopeful and needy as I was, and she was letting it show. Our whirlwind weeks were catching up to us. There was something that hung underneath the sweetness and recklessness of how we'd fallen together: a reminder that this wasn't a game. This was a cliff, and we were both losing our balance at the edge.

Frankly I would have let her push me.

"Yes." I answered, probably too quickly and eagerly. "Yes, definitely."

Madison's face brightened with a smile. She picked up my iced coffee from the cupholder and reached over to hand it to me.

"Go. I'll text you when I'm coming tonight."

I took my coffee and shut the passenger door, flashing her a grin through the window before jogging to the pool entrance.

As I stepped past the gate, I ran into Gigi, my shoulder hitting hers. I let out a laugh and fixed my backpack on my shoulder.

"Are you on with me today?"

She didn't answer right away. Her forehead wrinkled like she might scold me.

"What? Are you?"

"Did Madison Frank drop you off?"

I looked past the front gate, catching Madison's brake lights as she turned out of the lot. My eyes went back to Gigi. Her face hadn't softened.

"Yeah, she did. Why?"

"I thought you said you didn't hang out with her."

"I mean… I guess I do now."

I wasn't sure why I was lying to her again, so I resisted. I had to keep so much of my relationship with Madison secret, I wanted to be open about the parts I could. I couldn't read

Gigi's disapproval; I knew she wasn't Madison's biggest fan, but she was looking at me as if I'd smacked her in the face.

"Oh."

She shrugged, almost like she was trying to snap herself out of her own bad mood. I felt my face twist into the confusion I was feeling.

"I know you don't like her," I started. "But she's not really who you think."

"Dude, do what you want," Gigi said, putting both hands up, like she was recusing herself from the conversation. "For real. I don't care either way. But I warned you. So, you know. Be careful, I guess."

Gigi picked up her backpack, which had fallen by her feet. She shouldered it and backed away from me toward the gate.

"I'm off. Lindy's on for another hour and then I think you're on alone 'til three cause what's-her-name called out. But Liam's at the bar. See ya."

I sighed and watched her walk away, fishing out the keys to her old Corolla from her backpack's front pocket. Part of me wanted to go after her and explain—I didn't *need* to be careful. Madison was as nuts about me as I was about her. But I couldn't. And the larger part of me felt no need to defend my relationship with Madison. The larger part of me wanted to tell Gigi to mind her own fucking business.

I tossed my backpack into the duty room and tugged off the T-shirt I'd thrown over my guard suit. I took another sip of my iced coffee and realized Madison had handed me hers instead of mine, the taste of her Chapstick lingering on the straw. I felt warmth move through my limbs, a rush of eagerness and loneliness all at once. I left the cup in the duty room and grabbed my whistle, twirling it around my finger as I wandered out to the deck.

It was pretty crowded. The pool was busy with screaming kids and adults trying to swim laps around them. The deck was littered with moms and nannies and bored dads, the cabanas all claimed by groups of teenage girls. One of the groups was familiar—Madison's friends. They looked bored and aloof and beautiful in their Free People and Missoni bikinis, all ignoring one another to stare at their phones. I wondered if Madison would come by later and fit herself into the center of them, playing her role of queen bee while shooting me hungry glances from behind her sunglasses.

Liam waved at me as I passed the bar. He was in the middle of making four mai tais for two waiting women, both wearing the same Lilly Pulitzer beach tote on their shoulders. I saluted him playfully and headed to the guard chair, climbing up and heaving out a sigh as I dropped into the uncomfortable plastic seat. There was a palpable annoyance starting to settle on my shoulders. I didn't want to be at work. I wanted to be with Madison. I could feel myself weaving my entire existence into hers, doing the exact things I swore I'd never do again after Greer. After Philly. After Stone Harbor. After I'd lost myself so badly that I almost didn't come back from it. When we first left Philly for Willow Creek, I felt like only my body had taken the trip. Like I'd left my entire consciousness back in Philly—pieces of it where I'd stood on Greer's front steps and screamed and sobbed, and pieces of it in Stone Harbor, where Emma had gripped my arm in the cold ocean water, her long red hair disappearing below the surface.

But it was all coming back to me, slowly but certainly. The closer I got to Madison, the hotter the burn of those memories became, threatening to engulf me. Anyone close enough to me would be a casualty of the flames.

"Elliot!"

One of the girls from the cabana of Madison's friends called out to the tall, broad form that had just walked onto the pool deck. I clocked him immediately—that definitely-played-high-school-football-looking guy, with dark brown hair that was effortlessly disheveled. His jawline could have cut glass. He was, without a doubt, the kind of guy I avoided like the plague back in Philly; they were usually Temple frat boys cruising the coffee shops in Bella Vista, trying to hit on high school girls.

I turned in the guard chair, pushing my sunglasses up to get a better look at him as he lumbered over to the girls, grinning at them. I noticed a tattoo of a circle with Hokusai's Great Wave in black and white inside on his right bicep. I remembered last year's AP Art History lesson on the print, how it compared the true mercilessness of nature with the weakness of humanity.

My stomach twisted in on itself. I doubted he had any fucking clue about the print's meaning, so its presence on his skin made me sick with its lack of awareness I thought of the girl he assaulted, faceless in my mind, a stranger, a ghost. I wondered if he'd had that tattoo when he'd hurt her. If he'd had it the last time he'd laid his hands on Madison. The thought of it felt like nails on a chalkboard.

I realized I'd been clenching my fist in my lap. My nails left red half-moons in the heel of my hand.

The tangle of girls in the cabana unwound and let Elliot inside, and he settled in the middle of them, shirtless, and leaned back on a chaise longue. I couldn't hear what he was saying, but the girls looked downright captivated. I watched one of them, Sienna, Madison had called her, pull her sheer bikini cover-up off one shoulder, offering Elliot a better view of her pretty brown skin. He drank it in, pushing his sunglasses up into his hair and leaning closer to Sienna, daring to let his fingertips run from her shoulder to her elbow, a grin slithering onto his face.

I stole a glance back at the pool, trying not to stare at him. But the sounds of the girls in the cabana practically cooing over him drew my eyes back.

The weight of what Madison had told me—her lie covering for him, letting him get away with what he did, allowing him to carry on with his star boy persona intact—settled on me. Her best friends were convinced of his innocence. Or maybe they were weak enough to fall for his shit. To melt into his eyes as he looked at each one like she was the only person on the planet. I wondered how many girls he'd left a mess of smeared

makeup and a panicked text to their best friend—i thought he
was a good guy.

I imagined jumping down from the guard chair and grabbing
a paring knife from the bar where Liam had been cutting limes.
Crossing to the cabana and watching Madison's friends scatter
as I buried the short blade into Elliot's neck. I imagined how
I'd stand back and watch him panic, how all the girls' screaming would sound like white noise.

The screaming. The fantasy playing in my head melted
into a dark memory, a pair of ghost-white arms breaking the
surface of black water. A scream bubbling up from the push
of a wave.

"Lottie!"

The shrill exclamation of those two syllables slammed me
back to reality. I whipped around in the guard chair, looking
back to the pool. Lottie's nanny was running toward the
pool from her lounge. It seemed like she was moving in slow
motion. I tried to lodge myself in my own body as my eyes
followed hers.

In the pool, a small mass hovered below the surface a few
feet in from the edge. The red polka dots on her one-piece
caught the sun through the water.

Lottie.

I was out of the guard chair and in the pool before I could
even think her name again. My knee hit the bottom as I
clumsily pushed to reach her small body. The seconds it took
me to wrap my arms around her, pull her up, and drag her out

of the pool and onto the deck felt like it took hours. Long, desperate hours. Like watching a car drive straight toward a wall, anticipating the sharp crunch of metal and explosion of glass, the mere expectation of impact painful.

Lottie's nanny collapsed to her knees beside me on the deck.

"Lottie! Oh my God, Lottie! Is she breathing?"

My limbs felt numb. Water dripped off my hair and onto Lottie. The panic sent me into autopilot, and I ran through the steps like a machine, the chaos around me bleeding into static.

Tilt the head back. Open and check airway.

Lottie wasn't breathing. Her chest was still.

Hands together, center of the chest, thirty compressions.

I locked my hands together, trying to focus entirely on the compression count, trying not to lose myself in the motion and madness forming around me. People were closing in on us, a barrage of shouts and gasps and whispers. The pool emptied as kids crawled out of the water, standing beside their mothers and dads and nannies, staring at us like we were acting out a movie scene. Like at any moment someone could call *cut* or switch the channel, and we'd all tumble back into the safety of mai tais and meaningless conversations.

28. 29. 30.

Two rescue breaths.

I pinched Lottie's nose, my hands shaking. I pushed two breaths into her mouth. Waited to feel her body respond, to hear her cough out the breath I gave and pull in one of her own, but nothing came. Lottie laid still, eyes closed, lips blue.

I wasn't sure how long I'd been pushing on her chest. How many breaths I had forced into her still lungs. My arms were starting to ache. Her lips were cold each time I pressed mine to them.

Lottie's nanny was in a heap beside me, sobbing loudly. Mostly, I heard my pulse in my ears. My body shook so violently that I could hardly keep up compressions.

Sirens screamed over the noise around me. I was still trying to make her breathe, still smashing my hands into her small chest when someone grabbed my arms and pulled me away.

"No. No. Lottie. Stop. I have to—"

"Tillie."

Liam gripped me tight. Moved me away from Lottie's body. I felt a scream force its way up from the bottom of my stomach, ending with a pained cry. I was shaking too hard to fight Liam's hold. Paramedics took my place over Lottie, blocking her body from my view as Liam pulled me farther back. He held me against him. I stopped struggling.

My mind filled with black water. I could feel it in my lungs, could feel Emma's hands on my arms as she gripped onto me while the water pulled at her. Her face disappeared below the surface. Emma's face, then Lottie's face. A broken film reel skipped in my head as Lottie's nanny let out a scream that sliced into my chest.

The paramedics had stopped doing compressions. Through the gap between their bodies, I saw Lottie, just as still, just as blue.

"I didn't do it," I heard my voice say, but I felt far away from my body.

"I didn't do it. I didn't kill her."

"Tillie, it's not your fault. It's…" Liam's voice broke.

One of the paramedics pulled a sheet from the gurney and unfolded it. She laid it over Lottie as her partner got on his radio, its sharp beeps and alarms echoing inside my head.

I shivered in Liam's hold, repeating the words over and over, a sick mantra to counter all the black water filling up my head.

"I didn't kill her. I didn't kill her."

Chapter Nine

I barely remember getting from the club to my house. It felt like I suddenly came to hours later in my bed, a pile of limbs on top of my unmade sheets. There were flashes of what happened in between—Liam's grip on me, my body curling tightly into the front seat of his car, the ride to my house with his stoic presence beside me while I cried and shook. I remember stumbling out of his car onto my driveway and throwing up, my stomach twisting sharply.

And then nothing until opening my eyes again in my bed. There was rain on the windows, and the room was darkened. Quiet.

Fingers moved through my hair, gently pushing it away from my face. Madison leaned against my pillows. My head was in her lap, and her fingertips slid down the side of my neck. She didn't speak right away.

It came back in broken pieces. Lottie, the cold pool water, the blue of her lips, the sheet that paramedic pulled over her small, still body.

I crumbled into sobs, curling into myself. It felt like the bed and floor had dropped out from under me, and I was falling, falling, falling, anticipating the hard smash to the ground but never reaching it, trapped in the lurch.

Madison shifted to lie down beside me, and I felt her wind me up in her arms, felt her lips press to my forehead, felt her grip tighten. Her hold the only thing breaking my relentless fall.

I spent a few long, aching minutes like that, sobbing into Madison's neck. It took some hard pulls of air into my lungs before I felt like I had enough oxygen again, until my chest could stop rattling. Madison eased back enough to lift her hand to my face and wipe my cheeks with her fingers, to tuck my hair behind my ear. She kept her eyes on me. I was so shattered, my edges so sharp and raw, but she didn't recoil. She didn't even look away.

"Lottie. She…" I shook my head. My words stuck somewhere in my throat. Madison kissed between my eyes, the tip of my nose, my cheekbone.

"You did what you could, Tillie. This wasn't your fault. I need you to hear me when I say this wasn't your fault."

I pulled in a deep breath, held it for a moment, trying to steady my pulse. Once I could feel the bed underneath me again, I rolled out of Madison's arms, pulling myself to sit up. I tucked my body into the corner of my bed against the wall and tugged my knees up to my chest. Madison gave me space. She sat up and crossed her legs, quietly watching me, waiting for me.

I rubbed my eyes roughly with the heels of my hands, pushing away the newest tears, sniffling.

"I wasn't watching," I started, wrapping my arms around my legs, hugging them tightly. "I wasn't paying attention to the pool. And she cried wolf so much that I...I don't know if I would have taken her seriously if I had been watching. What does that say about me? That I might have let her drown? Even if I'd had the chance to stop it?"

"Tillie, it happened so fast. She might've accidentally sucked in a lungful of water while playing one of her pranks. There's no way to know what could have happened. But what *did* happen isn't your fault."

I dropped my chin against my knees, staring at a shadow on the duvet, trying to focus on anything other than the film reel playing in my head. Another horror movie in which I was the monster. A memory.

"Madison. It can't be a fluke that...this is the second time someone has drowned right in front of me."

She didn't respond right away. She opened her mouth, but then pressed her lips together. I looked at her, then back to the duvet. I couldn't meet her eyes, not while the nightmare was replaying in my head.

It was last summer.

The last weekend before Labor Day.

After Labor Day, Stone Harbor would be a ghost town, a beach village with the last of its summer residents packing up and heading inland. Greer's family had a salt-bitten beach house on the marsh with a shoddy old dock that jutted into the muddy water, the ocean just beyond the seagrass and dunes. You could see it from the roof deck, and we would always go up there when it stormed to watch the ocean slam angrily into the shore. We'd trace the depth of it back to the black clouds at the horizon, count the lightning strikes until one struck too close, and we ran screaming and laughing down the steps and inside, shivering and wet.

Greer and I had spent almost every weekend that summer at the beach house, driving out there on Friday afternoons when the air in Philly got so thick and hot that we could barely breathe it in. With the summer winding down, we knew our trips to Stone Harbor were numbered. We were running out of weekends to spend at the beach house, tucked inside one of the bedrooms, memorizing every inch of each other's bodies. And me, careening into a quiet obsession with Greer, a love I could never find the edges of. An endlessly deep and wide pool of dark water with no ladder. And Greer was always standing outside it, dry and safe, asking me why I was drowning.

That day, when I walked out of my house and found Emma Charles in the passenger seat of Greer's Subaru, every bone in my body seemed to calcify. My limbs stopped wanting to move, something so much bigger than me screaming to turn around and stay home. To not throw my backpack into the back seat and crawl in after it.

I remember Emma draped out of the passenger window, her red hair falling in loose curls against her bare arms and shoulders. She was grinning at me, watching me from behind heart-shaped red sunglasses. A Cheshire Cat, daring me to follow the White Rabbit.

Emma and Greer had started hanging out toward the end of the school year. Emma was the near antithesis of Greer; she wasn't so much a queen bee as a scorpion, ruling over her kingdom of pretty girls and desperate boys with a penchant for viciousness that terrified everyone. We all knew Emma Charles, without so much as breaking a sweat, could turn the whole school against us with one text message. She looked like she had been drawn by a man—lithe and lean with a waist that pulled in and hips that pushed out just enough, not to mention a set of full, plush lips that she painted with her signature red lipstick, stark against her porcelain skin. She was a teenage dream if I'd ever seen one. But somehow, she was always in my nightmares.

She'd kissed me at a party at Jordan Russo's house back in freshman year. She'd pulled me into a hall closet and pressed her lips to mine, her hand holding the side of my neck. And once she pulled away, she whispered, "No one will believe you, anyway," before leaving me in the closet, a laugh echoing behind her.

When she set her sights on Greer, I felt like prey who'd heard the click of a hunter's rifle.

Greer had been my best friend since the start of freshman year when we met in homeroom and sank our hooks into one another, our survival instincts telling us to latch on to the first safe person and hold tight. Greer had spent middle school being mercilessly bullied, her body softer and heavier than those of the girls who ruled the eighth grade. I remember our first sleepover when she told me about the days she went without eating, the diet pills she ordered off the internet with her mom's credit card, and how she cried while getting dressed every morning, forcing the width of her hips and thighs into unyielding jeans. She told me about how she collapsed one afternoon after not eating for two days, how she'd woken up in the nurse's office, how she hadn't been coherent enough to explain her parents weren't neglecting or starving her, how they had opened a child welfare case on her. How her parents had forced her into an outpatient treatment program for eating disorders and how she had sat in group therapy sessions in a circle of girls with bone-width limbs and hollowed-out cheeks. How one of them had sobbed during a session and called Greer's mere presence triggering. She told me how she began to wish she had another body, how she started designing a new one in her mind, one that fit the mold of perfection she thought she had to embody.

When we hit sophomore year, I had already fallen in love with her. I had spent our whole first year as friends learning every bit of her that I could, taking every piece she offered and setting it neatly on a shelf in my mind, where I could admire it when we weren't together. And a month or so into sophomore year, while I was tucked beside her in her bed at another one of our nearly weekly sleepovers, I dared to touch her cheek, to scoot in closer, to let my leg slip over one of hers under the duvet. She let me, and she leaned into me, and I kissed her, a brush of nervous energy, all my limbs practically vibrating. I'd waited for her to pull away, to put space back between our bodies; instead, she kissed me again. And again.

I wasn't especially "out" at school back then. I hadn't ever denied it, but I hadn't ever owned it, given it a name. I always wondered why I had to, why those of us who weren't straight had to climb on top of a proverbial soapbox and scream our identity for everyone to hear, when the straight kids never did. I wasn't ashamed, but I was fifteen. I didn't know who I was, yet. I envied the kids who had found a home in their own skin, the ones who walked down the hallways with their identities proudly displayed on pins and patches. But even if I wasn't there, I had found a home by Greer's side, my arm looped through hers on the walk between classes. And even if the other kids at school didn't know what we did and who we were outside those walls, it was almost better that way. We could have our private universe, one without the weight of their gazes and expectations.

But it also meant we never gave our relationship a name, never called it exclusive or made promises to belong only to one another. And that's how Emma slithered her way between us.

I don't know why she picked Greer of all the hearts she already ruled. Maybe she saw her as a challenge, a new conquest. It happened slowly. I noticed them smiling at each other in the hallway, and then I would find Emma at our lunch table. Not long after, I'd call Greer to hang out, but I'd hear Emma's laugh in the background as Greer told me, gently, "Maybe later."

Although Emma stole more and more of Greer, we still had our summer together. We still had our weekends at the beach house, even if I had to share Greer's weekdays with Emma. I usually refused to join them, preferring to maintain the illusion that they were just friends, when really I knew it was more. I knew they shared beds, and I knew that Emma had tasted the soft, sweet warmth of Greer's lips and skin. I knew they spent nights tangled up the same way Greer and I did, but when it was my turn, I pretended mine was still the only body Greer's had ever known.

That Friday, seeing Emma in the passenger seat—my seat—felt like more than I could bear, all of me suddenly crumbling underneath it. Whatever strength I'd had to pretend that Emma Charles's mere existence didn't set me into a spiral was gone. I spent the drive to the beach house drafting my monologue in my head, the one I'd scream in Emma's face if I was forced to accept that she had the spot I wanted in Greer's life.

I held it together until the second night.

Emma had pulled a bottle of Everclear and a few packets of Crystal Light from her backpack, a devilish grin on her face.

Desperate for absolutely anything to distract me from the fire raging inside my chest, I went shot for shot with Greer and Emma, music pulsing from a Bluetooth speaker as we laughed and danced.

Then Emma proposed we play truth or dare.

"Truth," Greer half slurred, grinning coyly at Emma. I took a sip of my drink, red cup sweating in my palm.

"Hmmm…" Emma started, and I could practically see the gears turning behind her eyes, like she was about to pull the pin in a grenade and throw it directly between Greer and me.

"Okay." She proclaimed, sitting up straighter, eyes fixed on Greer. "Do you want to go out with Tillie? Or…me?"

The carpet under my bare legs suddenly felt like a pile of rusted needles. Every tiny movement I made sent a sharp stab through me. I watched Greer hesitate, watched her nervously laugh off the question before taking a long gulp from her cup. But Emma looked on insistently, lifting her eyebrows.

"Em, c'mon, that's a stupid question—"

"But a fair one," Emma interrupted. "Right, Tillie? You wanna know, don't you?"

I looked over Emma's shoulder into the kitchen. I thought of the drawer where Greer's parents kept the knives. Imagined pulling one out and burying it in Emma's neck.

I didn't move or speak. Emma rolled her eyes, her amusement melting into annoyance.

"Answer. You picked truth. Not answering would be just as bad—"

"Fine. Emma. I'd wanna go out with Emma."

The silence that fell over the three of us was sharp enough that even Emma shut her fucking mouth. It didn't take long, though, for the smug smile to work its way back onto her face.

Greer avoided my eyes.

"Truth or dare, Em," she said quickly, before taking another hard gulp of her drink.

"Dare."

I was still trapped in the previous moment, the knife of Greer's admission stuck straight through my chest and into the wall behind me.

"I dare you to swim in the ocean, right now, in the dark."

Emma let out a laugh, threw back the last of her drink, and slammed her empty red cup on the coffee table. She stood up, still clad only in her tiny red bikini and an oversized zip-up hoodie.

"Hardly a dare. You think I'm scared of the ocean? C'mon."

We all walked the block to the deserted beach, our flip-flops smacking against the sandy pavement, hugging our sweatshirts close to us. Even with August still lingering, September was already pulling on the coastal air, the cool ocean wind blowing our hair behind us as we walked onto the sand.

Emma shrugged out of her zip-up and slid her feet out of her flip-flops, flashing Greer and me a grin before she took off running toward the waterline in a flash of red hair and laughter. I hung back with Greer, watching Emma jog into the small breaking waves, until she was far enough out to dive under another incoming push of water. I saw her resurface beyond the break, heard another laugh echo its way back to us on the shore.

"Hey, Til, I—"

"Forget it, Greer," I stopped her before she could start to apologize. I didn't want to hear it. I didn't want to listen to her try and explain why she would pick Emma over me. I already knew why. I'd just spent the last few months trying to pretend none of it was real, tricking myself into believing I had been anything more than an experiment.

I pulled my sweatshirt over my head and dropped it beside Emma's, leaving my sandals behind and walking to the water, wanting to put space between my body and Greer's. The water pulled at my ankles, cold and sharp, but I ignored the shivers already running into my limbs and pushed out farther, diving below the incoming waves to where Emma was treading just beyond them. In the bright moonlight, the white of her teeth glowed when she grinned at me.

"You're not scared either, huh?"

I looked back to shore at Greer's back as she stomped through the sand, back toward the street, back toward the house. Soon, I couldn't see her anymore. Emma and I were alone in the water, the waves gently pushing and pulling our bodies. I had already started to leave my own skin. I found myself hovering above the water, looking down watching myself as I swam closer to Emma, until we were close enough to reach out and touch each other.

"Do you remember Jordan Russo's party? Freshman year?"

My question made her grin again. She pushed her wet hair back with one hand and nodded, licking the saltwater from her lips.

"How could I forget that?"

I don't know what I was trying to accomplish, digging up the memory. I don't know what drew me to her, closing the distance until there were barely inches between us. My head was swimming with alcohol and false confidence, thoughts interspersed with visions of Emma and Greer tangled in Greer's bed. I saw Emma, mouth open, back arched, caught in a wave of pleasure. The film reel spliced with images of her bloody and gasping, her manicured red nails catching the light as she pulled a knife out of her chest.

Outside my own head, I was there in the water with her, watching her smirk at me. Outside my own head, I was moving my hand behind her neck, pulling her to me. She parted her lips before I'd even given her my mouth. The kiss tasted like saltwater, quickly deepening until we were pulling short breaths between pushes of our tongues' explorations. Emma's legs brushed mine as we tried to stay afloat. I bit her bottom lip, gathered a handful of her wet hair in my hand and pulled hard enough to break our kiss, to make her look at me, her kiss-swollen lips twisting up into a grin.

"You're so full of shit, Emma," I breathed, half winded from swimming and kissing.

I watched her smile fall. Her eyes darken.

"You don't want Greer. You want a plaything. Doesn't matter who. Case in fucking point."

She opened her mouth, poised to protest, but her words caught in her throat. She gasped, her shoulders sinking below the surface.

"Oh, fuck. My leg. I'm cramping—"

Another gasp, and she slipped below the surface, resurfacing with the next push of the ocean, sputtering saltwater.

"Tillie! Fuck, help me!"

I could have held on to her. I had already trained as a lifeguard at the start of summer—I knew exactly how to help. I could have wrapped my arms around her and pulled her toward the shore until her feet could find the bottom again. But I didn't. Instead, I pulled away when she grabbed for me. I put space between us as she fought the current and the pain, her reactions slowed by alcohol and exhaustion. I kept my head above water while she started to fight to stay afloat. When she grabbed for me again, I felt the sharp scratch of her red nails dig into my forearms as the water pulled her away from me. Pull her under.

I was out of my own body again, watching from above as I peeled her fingers off my arm. Pried my body out of her grip. And watched her take one more startled, terrified breath before disappearing beneath the surface.

There was one more flash of red hair under the water, a hard pull of another wave. My body pushed inland, my limbs loose and limp, letting the waves carry me toward shore. It

wasn't until my feet brushed sand again that my consciousness slammed back into me, knocking the wind out of me. I
heard myself gasping Emma's name, suddenly realizing none
of this had been a fever dream, none of it had been a trick
of my imagination, dreaming up ways to eliminate Emma
from the fucked-up equation of me and Greer. This was real.
I sucked in a hard breath, drops of saltwater getting caught in
my windpipe and making me cough as I tried to swim back out
through the breaks, my arms pushing desperately through the
water, searching for Emma.

I heard myself screaming her name, the two syllables getting
lost in the crash of the waves behind me, getting pulled away
into the strengthening wind. I dove under the water, opening
my eyes, seeing nothing but black. Still I reached, searched,
hoped to feel a brush of a limb in the darkness. But there was
nothing. Wherever the water had taken her, she was now out of
my reach. I scanned the surface again, nothing but moonlight
reflecting on the water. I fought the current, my arms and legs
aching, water in my mouth. I had to get back to shore before I
got swept away with her.

And so I did.

I crawled out of the ocean, coughing and gasping, my body
collapsing onto the sand once I was far enough from the pull
of the crashing waves. I lifted my head to scan the beach for
Greer, but she was long gone. She hadn't seen any of it. She
had no idea what had happened. Or how it had happened.

I picked up my sweatshirt from the sand and pulled it on

over my shivering torso, my mind already mapping out the lie I would tell. The way I would write myself out of the story of what happened to Emma. Like a door closing, my mind shut itself, quickly putting up protective walls around my memory. I hid there until I actually believed I didn't know what happened to Emma.

I remember the heaviness of my steps on the sandy pavement as I walked back to the beach house. I remember staying in my wet bathing suit and sweatshirt and curling up on the couch in the living room. I remember seeing Emma's red lipstick smudged on the rim of the glass she'd left on the coffee table. I remember falling asleep, only to awaken hours later to Greer's panicked voice calling out for Emma as she searched the rooms of the house for her. How I'd told her I had left her at the beach, how Emma hadn't wanted to come back with me. How she was still swimming when I walked away. I remember following Greer down to the beach in the pale morning light that painted everything gray, a haze drifting off the ocean and onto the shore. I remember Greer picking up Emma's sweatshirt and flip-flops from the sand where she'd left them the night before. I remember Greer collapsing onto her knees and how I'd watched from a few yards back, my eyes mapping the space between Greer and where the waves had washed away any trace of our footprints. I thought of what it might have looked like if they had remained—two sets of eager prints leading into the water, and only one coming out.

The cops called in the coast guard, and we watched as boats scanned the breaks for signs of Emma. Her parents showed up in Stone Harbor by the afternoon, and I watched them stand stone-faced on the pavement of the beach line next to a police cruiser, her mother holding a cardigan tight around herself.

Emma had run away before, a few times. She'd disappear and turn up in New York or DC a few days later, serve a few days of lockdown at her house before her parents freed her from under their thumbs, and she was free to do it again. I knew her parents were hoping that's what had happened this time too. I knew her mother was waiting for Emma's text, a photo of her standing on the deck of the Staten Island Ferry or drinking a coffee by the Reflection Pool. A train ride later and she'd be home again, laughing at her mother's worry, grinning while Greer rolled her eyes and said, "You really fuckin' scared everyone, you bitch."

I thought so hard about it—Emma in New York, sneaking into an off-Broadway show, or in DC, stepping off the trolley on H Street—that I started to believe it. To wait for her to resurface, to show up in Philly, Greer's phone to light up: *i'm back.*

But weeks went by. Long, quiet, aching weeks. School started with a heaviness hanging over the days like a fog over the ocean. Emma's friends cried in little huddles between classes. They held a vigil for her, asking for everyone to stay positive, to wish Emma home safely. And I stood near the back of the group gathered at Hawthorne Park, palms sweating as I

clutched the plastic handle of a little tea light in a cup, wishing
away the taste of saltwater from my mouth.

It was October when they found her body. It showed up in
the marshes in Brigantine, swept into a protected wildlife area,
laid to rest in the seagrass. I didn't know about it until I saw it
on the news. Local Missing Girl Found Dead.

I walked straight to Greer's. She came outside and stood on
her front stoop and stared at me. She looked so exhausted, so
tired of being sad. When I reached for her, she broke down,
sinking onto the top step and screaming, a sound so sharp I was
sure blood was dripping from the hole it put through my rib
cage. But I remember that I couldn't tell if the scream was from
pain or anger. Or maybe even fear. And I remember wondering, as I stood there on the sidewalk—people passing by and
pretending not to see her sobbing and screaming—if maybe
some part of her knew. If maybe she knew what had happened
that night after she walked away from the beach. If maybe,
just by looking, she could see the shadow that followed me.

Greer didn't come back to school after Thanksgiving
break. By then, we'd stopped speaking. We hadn't talked to
each other since that day on her stoop. I don't know why I'd
thought it would go the other way—that after Emma was
gone, and after the mystery of her goneness lifted, that Greer
would find comfort in me again. I'd imagined us back to how
we were before Emma stepped between us. Instead, the whole
ordeal had dropped us somewhere so far away from what
we had once been that I couldn't trace my footsteps back to

where we started. I couldn't even see the old us in the distance when I looked.

Greer transferred, enrolled in the private prep school all the way up in Chestnut Hill, so she wouldn't have to pass by our school in Bella Vista on the way, and she could leave behind every trace of me and her memories.

And that was exactly what she did. By the time school started back after winter break in January, I saw Greer posting photos of her new friends on her Instagram and Snapchat stories of them laughing at midnight at the diner we used to go to near Rittenhouse. Portraits of a happy new life she had fallen into so easily, like it was molded for her. We lived in the same city and yet it felt like Philadelphia had stretched out, fitting multiple universes inside itself, each bound by walls that kept them from ever merging.

And that was when I started to cave in on myself.

I didn't notice it happening right away. I didn't notice the way I slowly stopped speaking. Days would go by that I hadn't said a word, and it started to feel like I was forgetting how. I didn't notice the way I stopped eating, stopped doing my homework, stopped trying in my classes. I was sleeping through my alarms and missing days of school until the school administrator called my mom and threatened her with truancy officers. Mom held me on the couch crying and begged me to tell her what was wrong. I was too tired to cry with her, too tired to explain why I couldn't cry anymore. And eventually, after I had barely passed junior year, my mom announced she'd found a new job outside Philly and we were leaving. Starting new. Ripping off the Band-Aid of Greer and Emma and leaving behind our little row house on Mildred Street.

I remember being curled in the passenger seat of my mom's car as we followed the moving van out of the city, heading north on 309. I watched the towns pass outside the window, each one placing another few miles between me and the mess I made, and I started to let myself forget the sharpest pieces of the story.

Leaving Philadelphia, leaving Greer, I never imagined I would tumble into another bottomless ocean of a girl. Never thought I could feel as intensely as I had for Greer, not a second time, not another lightning strike in the same spot. But there I was, caught in the current of Madison Frank, happy to let her drag me away without a thought.

Madison sat in silence while I recounted the whole story. She watched me, her gaze never leaving me, although mine darted wildly while I told the story, occasionally spilling over with tears I didn't have the energy to fight. And even while I spilled my guts, I let her see every bit of me raw and honest and broken and fucked up. She never looked away. She didn't even flinch. Instead, once I had finished, she reached for my hand. I uncurled myself from my spot and the wall and laced my fingers with hers, my limbs unfolding to tangle with hers, letting her wrap me up in her arms and touch her lips to my forehead. It was the kind of wordless promise I was certain I'd never share with anyone again.

And then she pulled and looked at me, holding my face in her hands, and said the only thing that could have tied me to her even closer than I already was: "You didn't do anything wrong."

I committed it to memory as truth as it came from her lips. Bad things kept happening *to* me, not *because* of me. I wasn't a villain. I wasn't a killer. I was a girl. A girl who slipped too easily over every proverbial edge when some pretty girl made her feel wanted. And even as I was aware of it, even as I was trying to stop it from happening in the first place, there I was in the abyss of fixation and obsession over Madison. It had taken barely half a month for me to wrap every thread of myself around her. All that girl magic I had always believed in, I suddenly couldn't decide if it was saving me or ruining me. Maybe both.

Chapter Ten

I didn't go back to the pool after what happened.

The cops showed up at my house the day after and asked a hundred questions about it.

Were you watching the pool when it happened?

Were you the only guard on duty?

Did you see or hear Lottie trip or fall?

Did you hear screaming or struggling?

Did anyone else appear to hold Lottie underwater or push her in the pool?

That night after they left, I dreamed I was treading water in a rough ocean. A sharp undercurrent nearly pulled me below the surface, and I was fighting to stay afloat, to keep breathing. Dull, short fingernails dug into my arms. And as I struggled to peel back the fingers gripping my wrists, I saw

Lottie's face, staring up at me wide eyed from just under the surface.

I woke up screaming.

My mom took my keys and keycard back to the club. My boss sent me a single text: hope to see you next summer, stay well. But I knew she didn't want me to come back. How could I, anyway? And why would I want to? I never answered her text. I stopped answering everyone from the club. I was exhausted of hearing about it not being my fault. As people repeatedly told me not to blame myself and that it was an accident, I wondered how true that even was. Nothing felt accidental anymore. It all felt like pieces of an elaborate plan devised to destroy me.

July began quietly, a thick heat pulling over Willow Creek like a blanket, the days starting to last and last. Most mornings, my mom came into my bedroom to sit on the side of my bed and kiss my forehead, to check and make sure I was still breathing. She didn't push me to get out of the house or busy myself. I think part of her was happy to have me at home. She knew where I was at all times, even if I was in bed, the same few songs playing on a loop.

A few days into July, she came in to say good morning and laid down with me. She pulled me into her arms, and I let her hold me, let her cradle me like she did during the last time I was this broken. It made me imagine her at eighteen, with a tinier version of me zipped up inside her hoodie, fast asleep.

"Is Madison coming by today?"

She asked the question into my hair. Madison had been coming by every day since the accident. Sometimes she brought coffee, sometimes she stayed a while, sometimes she let me be alone with my grief if that was what I needed. She and my mom had at least met by then, and sometimes I would hear the two of them exchanging small talk in the living room. I knew my mom was still cautious. But as the days dripped by, she stopped questioning Madison so much and instead started to accept her as an ongoing player on the stage I'd set for myself here in Willow Creek. I think she would rather I have Madison than be alone, so she swallowed her doubts for my sake.

"I think so, maybe," I sighed, stretching my limbs and kicking off my duvet. Mom propped her head on her hand and gave me a small smile.

"How's that? You and her, I mean. It seems like her coming by is helping."

"Yeah, it is helping. I think. I guess. As much as it can, really."

Mom pushed her hand through my hair, and while she studied me, I could see her face soften, some of that anxiety about me leaving her features.

"She seems like a good addition to your life, Til. Just make sure to remember yourself."

There it was, a soft vibration under the surface of an otherwise calm lake. I gave her a nod and pressed my lips together in a thin smile. It was hardly reassuring, I knew, but it was all I could muster. She pressed another kiss to my forehead before she rolled off my bed and plucked a few stray piles of dirty clothes from the floor.

"I'm working an overnight tonight, so you're on your own for dinner. Cool?"

I gave her another nod, but she was already on her way out of my room, reminding me about not leaving clothes everywhere.

Once my door was shut, I pulled my phone from under my pillow and unlocked it. I hadn't looked at social media much since the accident, mostly ignoring it on the off chance I saw something about Lottie and spiraled. I opened Instagram and scrolled mindlessly through my feed for a few minutes, stopping to study photos of old friends from Philly enjoying summer days by the shore, influencers peddling protein shakes and body wraps, and the occasional friend of a friend going to birthdays and barbecues.

A box of *People You May Know* popped up. I recognized some of the faces and usernames—random club members, a nanny or two. But then there was one that sent a visceral wave of heat through my body: dark hair pushed carelessly back, a striking white smile, and that fucking Great Wave tattoo.

Elliot James.

I opened his profile and sat up in bed, my limbs suddenly restless. I scrolled through his posts—a collection of selfies and staged candids, most of them taken shirtless by a body of water. He had the kind of tall, cut physique that almost everyone who liked guys would lose their shit over. I skimmed some of the comments and found myself in a sea of pretty girls with cute usernames fawning over his every boring, predictable post. On a photo of him standing poolside at the club, **siennasayswhat** commented **@abercrombie, come get your new model.** On another photo of Elliot laughing and holding a Bud Light can, **juniebug** commented **what a smoke show.** I rolled my eyes and kept scrolling, fueled by only morbid curiosity and a growing urge to smash his perfectly proportional face into the pool deck.

I realized I'd scrolled too far when a photo of Elliot and Madison appeared on my screen. My insides tightened into a sickening knot. I recognized Madison's bedroom in the background, the bed where she'd first kissed me, just over Elliot's shoulder. He was suspended in a laugh, and Madison was half smiling, her gaze far away while they lounged on her sofa. It was dated before she said the assault took place, when she was still convincing herself that the charade wasn't eating her alive.

Before I could derail my own macabre thoughts, I was opening my browser app and typing *elliot james willow creek pa*. The first result was a photo of Elliot in the tracksuit all the dudes on the Willow Creek High boys' swim team wore. He was posing with a first-place trophy. The story under it had a glowing headline—*Willow Creek HS Student Breaks All County Record for 200 Yard Relay*. I kept scrolling, determined to find something—anything—that wasn't painting him like a hero. I finally found a single link from an anonymous question website that I remembered had been popular at my old school. The link took me to the page for username **eljamino**, which had a tiny photo of a smiling Elliot in the top corner. It took me a few moments of scrolling to see it, an anonymous question submitted around the time the assault had happened.

did u do it?

Underneath the question in stark black letters was: **that girl's a fuckin liar i never touched her**

In my head, I could see that grin he'd had at the pool the day of the accident and the way Madison's friends had draped themselves over him. A wolf in wolf's fucking clothing, and yet all the sheep were so entranced they never saw the sharp points of his teeth.

Another quick search yielded as few results: *willow creek hs pa sexual assault.*

I knew a newspaper wouldn't publish Elliot or the girl's names because they were both minors when the assault happened, but I thought they'd at the very least have covered the story. A small-town high school golden boy athlete accused of sexually assaulting a girl would have been huge news in Willow Creek. Only one story showed up. It was a short piece from a local newspaper with a simple headline: *Charges Dropped in Local Sexual Assault Case.* The article explained that "a local high school student" who had been accused of sexual assault was no longer facing charges after the complainant, a fifteen-year-old girl, recanted her statement.

I tried to imagine how it must have felt, sitting there in a police station, taking the truth back because the weight of everyone else's lies became too much to carry. Elliot's lies. Madison's. The burden of proving your own experiences was just one of the ways the broken, fucked-up system gaslighted victims. I'd read enough stories and seen enough episodes of *Law & Order: SVU* to know that the system was built to keep hurting people who have already been hurt.

A text popped up on my screen.

coming to pick u up tonight, be ready at 7.

Madison. The idea of leaving my bedroom cave was daunting; I hadn't put on clothing other than pajamas in days. But the prospect of getting into Madison's passenger seat was maybe the only thing that could convince me to do it.

I woke up from an unintentional nap at 6:30, my phone buzzing on my mattress. Texts from Madison littered my screen.

on my way
you better be up tillie gray!
be there in 20.

I liked each message and sent her a purple heart emoji before rolling myself out of my bed. In the time I had, I brushed my teeth, washed my face, threw my wild hair up into a bun, and pulled on a pair of shorts and a tank top. I knew the air outside was going to be hot and thick, the forecast predicting a heatwave for the next few days. I shoved some spare clothes and a toothbrush into my backpack, knowing that I would end up with Madison overnight, especially with my mom working. Mom had been taking day shifts since the accident—I hadn't wanted to be alone at night when the nightmares came. Her taking the night shift felt like a quiet nudge toward normalcy, even if I was still scared of what lived in my thoughts.

As I was dropping my phone charger into my backpack, my phone buzzed again.

outside.

I shut off the lights in the house on my way out and locked up behind me. Seeing the BMW idling in the driveway sent a shiver of excitement through me, one I hadn't felt in a while, one that settled in my chest like a warm pulse of happiness. If I let myself, I was going to lose sight of where I ended and Madison began. I was already starting to forget.

At 6:45, the summer sun was still high. Madison smiled at me from the driver's seat, as I climbed into the other side. An iced coffee was waiting for me in the cupholder.

"I was worried I would have to come in there and drag you outta your bed," Madison said, putting the car in reverse and whipping back onto the street. She headed toward the main boulevard and took the left toward the highway.

"My mom's working overnight tonight, so I was kinda happy to get outta the house."

"Oh good, so she won't mind if I keep you 'til the morning, then."

She flashed me a grin, and I caught myself staring at her profile while she drove for a few quiet minutes. From the route, I knew she was taking me to the lake house, but I wasn't complaining. Our time at the lake house was nothing short of sacred. Going home after being there felt like taking off noise-canceling headphones, all that angry sound rushing back in.

An exit or two down the highway, I remembered the sleuthing I'd done earlier and felt a grip of panic about bringing it up with Madison. I thought of the photo of her with Elliot, that lost, sad look on her face. I thought of the nameless girl, sitting in a police station, taking back her words.

"Can I ask you something...something you may not wanna talk about? It's okay if you don't want to answer."

Madison glanced at me, curiosity on her face. She shrugged one shoulder.

"I'm an open book," she answered with a little smile.

I hesitated. Took a breath.

"How come your friends still hang out with Elliot? I mean...even if they don't know the whole story, you'd think the allegations against him would be enough to make them fawn over him a little less."

I saw Madison grip the steering wheel a little tighter, then relax again. Her jaw set.

"Because they're not really my friends, Til. They're just... costumes I wear to play my role. Ever since I got back from boarding school, I've fought for my fucking life to fit the mold, to look and act how everyone wants me to, to tuck away all the bullshit that happened at boarding school and afterward deeper and deeper so that I don't have to deal with the fallout."

She stopped for a moment, adjusting her sunglasses, tapping her fingers on the wheel. I couldn't tell if they were nervous tics, or if she was fighting a more visceral response. I knew as well as anyone how needlessly cruel the politics of high school were, but I'd never felt the weight of them the way Madison did. Sure, kids got bullied and shit on for being gay in Philly too, but I knew it was different here. Smaller towns get set in their ways like a stubborn grandparent. People refuse to acknowledge that their fear of change isn't an excuse to treat others like they're broken and unworthy—which is, I know, exactly how Madison felt. Enough that she internalized it and spat it back at other people who were being treated the same way. Still, even when I handed her a shovel and she started digging, I knew there were other skeletons in that graveyard that she hadn't told me about. I knew there were bodies buried there, whose names she hadn't said out loud. Coffins full of crumpled, handwritten notes, every secret she refused to give voice to, nailed in. A pretty girl, whose name she wouldn't say out loud, disappearing past a tree line.

I reached across the center console and gently uncurled her fingers from the wheel, giving her my hand to hold on to, instead. I kissed the back of her hand, holding it between both of my own, my eyes fixed on her.

"You never have to pretend with me," I told her, the fingers on my free hand ghosting up her forearm and back down. "You're safe. I'd never let anyone hurt you. You know that, don't you?"

With each word I spoke, I saw her soften a bit more. She settled into her seat, loosened her one-handed grip on the wheel, and glanced in my direction.

"You know, it's probably insane on both of our parts that we're at this point already, but I keep realizing over and over that I truly don't care if it is insane. I might even be rooting for it to be."

The little smile that followed her words earned one back from me. She squeezed my hand.

"But for the record," I added as Madison switched lanes to speed around a slow-moving minivan. "I doubt you'll ever really need my protection. I'm sure you could take down anyone who tried to hurt you."

"You'd think," she said, flashing her middle finger at the minivan's driver as she sped past. "But I'm not the take-no-shit badass you might think I am. At least not when it comes to defending myself. Other people? Sure. I'd fucking run someone over for looking at you wrong. But me? I'd let myself get stepped on until I couldn't get back up again."

The image of it set something off in me. The first face that popped into my mind was Elliot James. And as we drove the next few exits in silence, I imagined jamming the sharp end of one of his swimming trophies into his gut.

By the time we made it to the lake house, the sun was starting to lower. The house sat waiting for us at the end of the long driveway, the lake spread out behind it.

"You feeling up to a little work before we call it a night?" Madison asked me as we got out, both of us shouldering our backpacks. "I have some lamps and flashlights we can take."

Putting my idle hands and mind to work on something purposeful felt like a good idea. I was already anxious to sit still and quiet for too long, the rush of ocean waves and the sharp chlorine scent of pool water ever present in the back of my mind, waiting for space to be let inside.

I followed Madison through the house, both of us grabbing things we needed along the way: some battery-powered lamps and flashlights, the extra cans of sky-blue paint sitting by the back sliding glass door, and a soft cooler filled with spiked seltzers from the fridge. Madison plucked the boat key off the wall by the door, and we ran down to the dock, the thick evening air catching our laughter and carrying it out over the water.

I watched Madison while she maneuvered the boat along the curve of the lake, picking up enough speed to push the wind through the loose baby hairs at the nape of her neck, her sunglasses pushed on top of her head. By this point, the simple routine of riding out to the old dock at the cemetery was becoming muscle memory. I jumped out to help tie up the boat, then I offered my hand and helped her up onto the dock. Once she was close to me, she touched a kiss to my lips, and I felt her smiling into it.

We carried our things through the woods, the sun still up high enough to light our way through the tree canopy, late evening summer beams of orange and red pushing through the cracks in the leaves and down to the pine needles that littered the ground. We followed the path dutifully, quiet aside from the crunching of our steps. When the cemetery materialized in the clearing, we set everything up, Madison opening the front door of the playhouse to take out the tools we left there from before.

I got to work first on opening and stirring the paint. Last time we'd come, we'd taken down the shutters and sanded and primed them, following the steps from her hours of YouTube research. Madison began painting the front door. Instead of painting it the same sky blue it had been, Madison had chosen a stark red. I watched her paint, the sudden splash of red seeming bright even in the steadily darkening light.

After getting a coat of blue on one of the shutters, I walked around to turn on all the battery-powered lamps, giving us more light to work with as the evening wore on. We were always content to work in the quiet, music playing softly from Madison's phone, comfortable in the silence we shared. But today, I had something under my skin. While I set the first shutter against a nearby stone to dry and began painting the next one, all I could think about was Elliot James. He'd been occupying undeserved space in my mind since the day of the accident, that sick smile he'd been wearing right before it happened still haunting me. That day's deep dive into his social media hadn't helped. It felt like I was continuing to throw kindling on the growing fire inside me, a fire he'd ignited. A fire, I was realizing, that might only be extinguished by extinguishing Elliot himself.

"Hey, Mads?"

Madison didn't look away from the door, still painting it in careful, steady strokes.

"Hm?" She answered.

"Elliot James doesn't deserve to keep living his life like nothing happened."

I said it matter-of-factly, dipping my brush into the blue paint. I heard Madison shift where she was kneeling in front of the playhouse.

"No. He doesn't."

I looked over at her, both of us paused in our work, the lamps casting a soft glow on Madison's features. After a moment, she set her jaw, then dipped her brush, wiped it along the side of the paint can, and kept working.

"What're we gonna do about it, though?" She finally added. I could tell from the steadiness in her voice that she wasn't asking in defeat—she was asking because she wanted an idea.

I laid my brush over the top of the paint can and thought. I thought about the sharp end of that swimming trophy again.

I thought of the hard pull of a nighttime ocean, the flashes of Emma's pale face replaced with Elliot's, his hands the ones grasping for help as I shoved his thick shoulders under the surface.

"I don't know yet," I said, looking at her. "But I'm gonna do something."

"*We're* gonna do something."

Her correction made me lift an eyebrow at her, and I felt my mouth twist into a smirk. She mirrored it back at me and returned to her work.

An hour or so later, when it got too dark, even with the help of the lamps, we put the lids on our paint cans and stacked them inside the playhouse. On the walk back to the dock, Madison held my hand, her fingers laced with mine, our flashlight beams bouncing on the pine needles in front of us. The hum of katydids and crickets seemed softened by the thick humidity in the air, the night hanging over us like a blanket tossed over the treetops.

I helped Madison untie the boat from the dock, jumping in beside her as we pushed off. She took us around the bend and back out into the open part of the lake before killing the engine. It was a clear night, and that far outside town, we could see every star, the sky dotted with bright pinpricks, the moon bright enough to cast shadows of our silhouettes onto the floor of the boat.

Madison pressed the winch button to drop the anchor. The water was still enough, though, that we probably could have floated there all night without moving too far. I stood by the front end of the boat, watching Madison, my eyes following the outline of her form as she turned back to face me. She smiled, starting to move toward me, until I reach out my hand and she caught it, drawing me to her. We stood in the boat, the moon lighting our faces, and I took that moment to memorize hers, its soft curves, the dimple on one cheek, the tiny scar on her chin from when she'd fallen off her bike as a kid, a story she'd told me on one of our nights tangled in her bed.

I felt her arms circle my waist, and I followed her lead, hooking mine around hers, our foreheads leaning together as we started to slowly sway to the soft music still coming from her phone, which had been dropped onto the boat's steering console. I knew, in that moment more than ever, that I was ruined. I was a skeleton stitched together with needle and thread. I knew in that moment that she was, somehow, simultaneously the sickness and the cure. I wanted to live in our secret moonlit world, forever weightless on the surface of Hidden Lake, forever devastated and elated in the same breath.

"I think…" Madison started, our bodies still swaying. "I think that this could destroy me."

She spoke the words on the tip of my own tongue. I gave her a nod, our foreheads still touching, my arms tightening around her.

"I know." It was all I could muster. She also nodded, and then kissed me, an *amen* to a silent prayer.

Chapter Eleven

I had time to spend with Madison now that Mom was back on night shifts and couldn't spin her helicopter blades above my every move. I would watch my mom's car back out of the driveway and wait for Madison's BMW to replace it moments later, the glowing porch lights signaling her in. We became nocturnal creatures, living in the dark, falling asleep after dawn, and sleeping until the afternoon. We spent the next week driving around the streets of Willow Creek at night, running red lights through deserted intersections, screaming the lyrics to the songs we loved with the windows down. We'd park in the lot outside the vacant strip mall over by the highway on-ramp, lay the front seats back, and open the sunroof, staring up at the clouded night sky and telling stories about our lives in the Before—before I showed up there in Willow Creek, before Madison shed Elliot like a snakeskin.

One night, it rained. The sky hadn't seen a drop in what felt like weeks, but when it finally fell, it fell hard, soaking our nighttime town.

We were parked in an empty lot of the little downtown strip in Willow Creek, all the shops and restaurants closed. The only spot still showing signs of life was the dive bar about a block up, the occasional patron jogging from the door to their car through the steady rain. We rarely came down to Main, no matter the time of day. It was too much of a threat to the privacy of our little universe. Even one pair of unwelcome eyes would be a lot.

I wasn't sure why Madison had chosen to go there that night. She'd picked me up an hour earlier, and I'd thrown my body into the passenger seat with a laugh, but Madison had only smiled. She'd been quieter than usual. I could practically see wheels turning behind her eyes with whatever was on her mind.

It wasn't until she'd given up crisscrossing the town and settled for the lot on Main that I decided to break the gentle tension of the quiet.

"You're thinking about something."

I stated, rather than asked, her about it. I knew she would drag me through the loops of her mind like a cat chasing a toy before finally letting me in. Madison had her knees pulled up to her chest in the driver's seat, and she rested her cheek on them, looking over at me. She studied me for a long moment, and I watched the shadows from the rain streak down her face and bare arms.

Finally she nodded. I waited. Pulled my knees up to my own chest and laid my cheek against them, mirroring her body. For a split second, I saw Greer, smiling across from me in the Subaru, the front seats laid back, her hand reaching across to me. I forced Greer out of my mind, focusing on Madison, eyes mapping the curves and shape of her in the driver's seat, grounding myself.

"I'm thinking about what you said back at the playhouse. That you wanted to do something about Elliot James."

Something clicked inside me when she said his name. That pilot light, flickering back to life. I thought of that photo of him grinning in his swim team uniform, the pages of local news praising him, Madison's friends encircling him like he was a deity. The lines forming the Great Wave on his shoulder, symbolic only of his own destruction.

"I *do* wanna do something about Elliot James," I said. "I just don't know what. He seems untouchable, like nothing we could do would actually affect him."

She looked at me for another moment before looking back out the windshield, her eyes fixed on the door to the dive bar up the block. The rain was starting to let up against the roof of the car.

"I don't care if it doesn't have the consequences he deserves," she said. "I still want to hurt him."

Hearing her frankly say those words sent my stomach into a backflip. I knew my own urges to hurt Elliot James were just as real, just as visceral, but hearing Madison voice the words that had only been bouncing inside my brain felt like plunging down a sharp drop on a roller coaster.

I expected, in that moment, to be back in that nighttime ocean, to feel the sting of Emma's grip on my arms, to taste cold saltwater in my mouth. But I didn't. The ghosts of that night stayed outside the car, and I ignored their tapping at the windows. Instead that pilot light caught to full flame, Madison's words that *click-click-click* before the gas.

"So," I said, my eyes still fixed on hers. "We'll find a way to hurt him."

Madison dropped her legs and leaned across the center console, catching my lips with hers. I felt her fingers grip the back of my neck, the sharp sting of her nails digging in as she kept me locked in that kiss—as if I would have pulled away for anything short of a tidal wave.

She was shifting her body, preparing to crawl over into my lap, when movement outside the bar caught both of us. We craned our necks to see through the half-fogged windshield, the rain having let up to barely a sprinkle, giving us a better view.

Elliot James had stumbled out onto the sidewalk, flanked by two guys who looked like they'd been manufactured in the same batch as Elliot. The same swath of dark hair, the same broad shoulders, same T-shirt printed with some fraternity letters or another. The pieces slowly fell into place—why we'd parked here, why she'd been so focused on the bar. I looked across the street and saw what I guessed was Elliot's car, a newer-model Audi something-or-other, parked along the sidewalk. My eyes went back to the boys, then to Madison, whose pulse I swore I could see thudding in her throat.

Even I knew, in all my impulsiveness and desire to fuck with Elliot, that this wasn't the time. Not when he had henchmen. Not when there would be witnesses. But I didn't know what Madison was thinking. And she was staring at Elliot like she was cursing him.

"We can't now," I said out loud. "Not with those dudes with him."

"Tyler and Blake? Spineless pricks. Both of them. They know the truth."

I looked at the two clones following him Elliot the sidewalk, all moving slowly, captured in conversation and laughter. I saw flashes of visions—the paring knife on the bar at the club buried in his neck, the sharp end of a swimming trophy swung at the side of his perfect face. But before I could say anything else, Madison paled. I saw her eyes widen and followed her gaze back across the street. Elliot's two friends were talking animatedly on either side of him. But he wasn't listening to them. He was staring at Madison's car, a smirk slowly crossing his face.

She got out of the car before I had time to think. She was so ready to ruin him that she'd forgotten the power he had to do it right back—again. I hurried out of the passenger side after her, both of us on a hair trigger, her ready to go after him, and me ready to go after her. She didn't move, simply watched him intently, her jaw set, like she was daring him to take a single step toward us.

I was so busy watching Madison that I didn't see Elliot when he started to laugh. Then he started a slow, pandering clap and stepped to cross the street. His two friends looked at each other, like they were trying to decide if they should stop him. Elliot was clearly drunk, his steps wavering, half stumbling off the curb and into the empty street.

"Madison fucking Frank," he said, each word punctuated with another hard clap of his hands. "Fancy seeing you here."

"Don't you have enough DUIs, Elliot?" Madison said, her voice shockingly calm. "Shouldn't you stop fucking up before your daddy takes away your car?"

He let out another laugh. It grated against my ears. My fingers curled into fists, nails digging into the heels of my hands.

"Shouldn't *you* stop running around town with girls?" He shot back. "Wouldn't want anyone to get the wrong idea about you, now, would you, baby?"

My eyes went from Elliot back to Madison and I saw her close her mouth, stopping herself before she could say anything to that.

"And...this girl, of all girls?"

Elliot's voice drew my eyes back to him. He was staring right at me now. My stomach flipped, twisting into a knot of anger. I wasn't afraid of Elliot James. That drunken, overgrown idiot swaying in the street, sneering at Madison and me wasn't intimidating, despite his best efforts. To me, he looked like an annoying mess to clean up.

"Really, Maddie?" He went on. "You're gonna go around with this bitch? The girl who let that kid die at the club?"

As the words came out of his mouth, it was like the ground shifted under my feet. Like the earth between him and us was about to open and swallow us whole. The anger I had burning hot in my belly iced over at the mere mention of Lottie. My eyes blurred with tears, and I tried not lose my spine at one backhanded comment. But all that dark water came rushing in, and I felt it wash over my feet, saw it flooding the street between us, and I knew I was seconds away from going under. From drowning.

I may have felt paralyzed, but Madison wasn't. His words, for her, had been a catalyst, a slingshot, a kick start. She started forward, poised to stomp her way across the street to him. Something told my legs to move, and I forced my way through the thick black water that was weighing down my limbs to grab her. I held her arm and pulled her back, stopped her from stepping off the curb and into the street. In my head, the water was still rushing in. I needed her to make it stop. I needed her to come back into her body to get me out of there.

He let out another laugh.

"What are you gonna do, Maddie? Huh? You never did anything before. Well. At least not to me. Can't say the same for everyone else."

All at once, Daisy's name dug itself out of its burial plot in my head. My grip on Madison's wrist tightened.

Madison spat into the street in Elliot's direction.

"You're a piece of shit."

I hadn't seen her wrapped so tightly in anger before. I hadn't seen the way it roped itself around her neck and left her a tense knot, her body spring loaded and ready to leap forward at any moment.

"You never used to say that," he started, grinning sickly, and I was already pulling on Madison's arm, making her back up. "But I guess your mouth was a little busy when we were together, huh?"

Madison yanked her arm free of my grip in one sharp pull, and before I could even follow what was happening, she had crossed the street and swiftly smacked Elliot across the face.

In the time it took me to go after her, I saw Elliot recoil and draw his hand back, ready to hit her back. His friends quickly stepped in and grabbed both of his arms, yanking him away before he could land a blow.

"She's not worth it," one of them coaxed. "Let's get out of here."

I hooked my arm around Madison's middle, and this time, she didn't fight my hold. I could feel her uneven breath against my arm.

As Elliot's friends tugged him back onto the sidewalk, he rubbed at his jaw and gave us another dark grin, chuckling to himself.

"You two run along now," he chided, his friends pulling him toward one of their cars. "Try not to kill anymore little kids, yeah?"

Madison and I stood on the wet street and watched Elliot's friends get him into the back seat of one of their cars. As they pulled off the curb, Elliot was grinning at us from the window.

The street fell back into silence. The only sound I heard was Madison's still-labored breath and the hushed sound of the rain that had started again, softly pattering on the pavement. Madison calmly took her keys out of her pocket, and I released my hold on her, ready to leave with her. But instead of walking back to her car, she stepped up to Elliot's Audi, which was still parked on the curb. With barely a glance in either direction, Madison dug her car key into the driver's-side door. I felt myself recoil at the harsh scratching sound as she carved the word RAPIST into the black paint.

She stepped back, examining her work. Apparently satisfied with it, she turned back to me, her face was wet with tears. But they didn't look like sad tears—they looked like angry tears. I could feel the dark ocean water pulling at my ankles, the smell of chlorine thick in the air.

Back in the BMW, Madison turned the car key in the ignition and put the car in drive, turning to me before she let off the brake.

"I want to ruin his fucking life," she said firmly.

I nodded. "Then we will."

Chapter Twelve

A couple long, heavy weeks after the accident, Gigi showed up at my house.

It was late afternoon. I'd just woken up and was perched on the couch with a bowl of cereal while my mom got ready for work down the hall in her room. I knew Madison wouldn't show up until Mom left for work, so the unexpected knock made me jump. I set my bowl on the coffee table and hurried to the door, peering through the peephole. The shock of seeing Gigi standing there was quickly replaced with a rush of relief. Until that moment, I hadn't realized that I'd assumed she was done with our friendship.

I opened the door and Gigi smiled. I returned it, then let out a laugh.

"What're you doing here, Gi? I've missed you."

And I did. I had missed her. I missed a lot about my life before the accident, the simple, easiness of a life I was only just starting to build and live before I needed yet another fresh start.

"I...I was on my way home from the club, and I hadn't heard from you in a while, so I...here I am."

She shrugged, wringing her hands. I stepped aside, gesturing into the house.

"C'mon. Come in. Let's go out back and talk."

Gigi followed me through the living and dining rooms and out the slider in the kitchen. Mom and I hadn't done much to the backyard yet, but we had a covered deck with a little porch swing that we both loved, so I took Gigi over to it. We both fell into the swing's cushions, and I pulled one knee up to my chest, my other foot on the ground, gently swaying us.

"How is everything at the club?"

As I asked, I wasn't sure I really wanted to know. It didn't matter if most people didn't blame me, or even if most people had moved on. I blamed me. And I hadn't moved on from what had happened.

Gigi shrugged again, gently swinging one of her legs.

"Exactly the same. Same stuff every day. Oh, except that Liam quit."

"Liam quit? Why?"

"I don't know, I guess he wanted some time to himself before going to school next month."

I remembered the last time I saw Liam. How he'd carried

me away from Lottie's covered body, tucked me into his car, took me home. I still had his sweatshirt that he'd pulled over me before my mom had gotten home and relieved him from looking after me that afternoon.

"Good for him, although I'm not sure how he's gonna live without all that unsolicited flirting from those middle-aged club moms."

Gigi chuckled. "Yeah, right? He might wither away without the attention."

We both smiled and fell back into silence. A warm breeze rustled through the trees. I swatted a fly from my leg. I had a feeling we were both circling through the same thoughts, trying to decide which things to carefully avoid bringing up.

It was Gigi who gave up first.

"How are *you* though, Tillie?"

I forced a tight-lipped smile. I knew it probably looked sadder than if I had not smiled at all.

"I mean," I started, then stopped. I shrugged one shoulder.

Gigi nodded.

"Yeah," she said, looking back down to her hands in her lap. "I figured as much."

"It's been getting better, you know? I gotta force myself out of my own head sometimes, but at least I've had some good distractions."

I thought of Madison and wondered if she'd text me. My phone was inside on the couch. I had a feeling she was still asleep, shut away in the dark quiet of her bedroom, waiting for her parents and brother to vacate the house before she dared emerge.

"You mean Madison Frank."

I was half shocked to see her smiling after mentioning Madison. I knew Gigi wasn't Madison's biggest fan. I remembered her warnings, the way she'd seemed so frustrated by my willingness to be and stay in Madison's immediate orbit despite those warnings.

I was trying not to be too obvious about how the mention of Madison sent my insides into a gymnastics routine. But without Madison, I wasn't sure I would have made it through those first days after Lottie.

"She's...been a really good friend to me. I know you don't care for her—"

"I only told you that stuff because I didn't want to see you get hurt," Gigi interrupted. "If she's been good to you, which it seems like she has, then it's a moot point."

I nodded, and I let silence settle between us again. Gigi and I swung gently for a few moments before I let my mouth form the question I had been trying to swallow back.

"Hey...what do you know about Elliot James?"

Gigi looked at me, half confused.

"You mean, other than the fact he's the douchebag who used to date Madison?"

I nodded, letting my question stand. Gigi pressed her lips together and shrugged, sighing.

"Well, not a whole lot, I guess. He graduated this spring

and is going to Temple in the fall, cause his dad and brother did or something. He always made a huge deal about being some kind of shoo-in legacy. I know he was on the swim team. And I know he really did hurt that girl."

Her last sentence caught me. I wet my lips and pressed them into a tight line, resisting the urge I had to confirm her beliefs, and instead trying to recalibrate my line of questioning, so I could get as much information as possible from Gigi without setting off her alarm bells.

"What all do you know about that?" I pushed.

This time Gigi hesitated to answer. I kept my eyes on her, silently willing her to say whatever she was visibly trying not to.

"She was someone I knew. Not well, but she was an acquaintance. We had a class together before it all happened. She was a freshman, and she was taking yearbook with me. I heard the stories everyone else heard. There was a party at Tyler Dennison's one weekend, and a ton of people from school were there. It was fall of last year—October, I think. Around homecoming week. Elliot was a senior hitting on a freshman girl, and I'm sure you can guess that he has the insanely undeserved privilege of making everyone he pays attention to fall in love with him."

I felt myself cringe. Gigi made a face in agreement before she continued.

"So she was smitten with him. I guess she had been for a while before this happened. Around that time, I remember Madison making fun of some freshman girl who thought she had a chance with Elliot. Someone told me later that at the party, he took her upstairs, but she was pretty drunk. No one knows for sure what happened upstairs, but some of her dumb friends dumped her—passed out drunk—on her own front lawn afterward. Her parents took her to the ER when they found her, and at the hospital, she told them she'd been assaulted. At least, this is what I heard. Administration made a pretty public statement at school. They sent out this email to everyone's parents about the dangers of drinking or whatever. And in that email, they said something about a student being assaulted at a private party over the weekend and that the school was working with law enforcement in the investigation.

"That confirmed the rumors for everyone, even though they never said the girl's name outright. Then Elliot's shitty friends went to bat for him, telling the cops and the school that they knew for certain he hadn't been near the girl. Madison backed him up too, but I never could understand why—everyone said she wasn't even at the party."

I felt my jaw clench. I was imagining it again—Madison sitting in the precinct, hands twisting in her lap, sweat on her neck as she lied to protect herself from more of the harm that shitbag had already caused her. I knew the guilt Madison felt, how heavy it weighed on her. But that was her story to tell, not mine. As badly as I wanted to defend her right then, I knew there was a bigger picture I needed to consider. Plans to reset the scales back in her favor.

I nodded, and chewed the inside of my cheek, thinking. Gigi kept going.

"Why do you ask? Did Madison tell you something different? I mean, she and Elliot broke up shortly after that, so it's hard to not think that had something to do with it."

I shook my head, trying to backpedal.

"They broke up because he was a dick to her," I explained, picking my words carefully. "He used to be really mean to her and call her names and stuff when they were together. I think she reached her breaking point."

Gigi nodded slowly, and I could tell she was trying to decide if she believed me.

"I was morbidly curious, I guess," I said, anxiously filling the silence. "I saw him at the pool back when I was still working, and I saw all of Madison's friends being all buddy-buddy with him. It made me wonder what his story was. It seems like someone who does something like that...should face consequences."

"Yeah, you'd think, huh? But no. Not kids like Elliot... Those douchebags are untouchable around here. Part of me hopes they'll all get a rude awakening when they get to their fancy private colleges and realize no one gives a shit who they are, but I know better. They'll be worshipped there too. The whole system is built to benefit them. The whole world is."

There was an edge to Gigi's words that I didn't recognize. I caught her gaze again and nodded slowly, taking in a deep breath. I could understand her anger about this particular situation to a point—we both lived as women in a world built to the benefit of men. But I thought of Gigi's parents, speaking their home language to each other behind the counter at their coffee shop. Her mom had once taught me how to say *yeppeuda*—beautiful. She wrote the Korean characters on a napkin, touching each as she pronounced it. *Yeppeuda*. The next time we went to the shop together, her mom wrote those characters on my cup instead of my name.

I thought of the careful ways they probably had to navigate our small American town. The town was insular, and some people could be more than a little closed minded. People often mistook their racism for mindless patriotism. On one of our drives, Madison and I had passed a house off one of the back roads with a flag out front that read BUILD THE WALL. I tried to imagine Gigi and her parents serving those people coffee. I knew, without a doubt, that they still smiled as they did it.

I understood now, as I sat there quietly swinging back and forth with Gigi, why Madison had made the choices she did.

"Well, I gotta help my parents close up the coffee shop," Gigi said. "But I'm really glad you're okay, Tillie."

Gigi leaned over and wrapped her arms around me, hugging me tightly. I wasn't used to Gigi's affection, but the way she held on to me made me squeeze her just as hard in return, suddenly recognizing how much I'd needed it.

"Text me, okay?" She added as a goodbye before she stood up and gave me a little wave, stepping off the deck and disappearing around the side of my house.

I stayed there, swaying on the back porch swing, running everything Gigi told me back through my head. I wasn't sure if I had been looking for a reason not to go after Elliot or for more reasons to do exactly that, but I'd gotten the latter. It was becoming abundantly obvious that Elliot James had no redeeming qualities. There was nothing I could find that was changing my mind on the fact that he deserved to be punished. That he'd never been punished or held accountable for anything before and that it was overdue.

He had it coming. Just like Emma.

Chapter Thirteen

It had been an unfortunately timed text message that had tipped Elliot off about Madison. She was retelling the story while we painted the playhouse later that week, both of us carefully layering fresh white paint onto the siding we'd sanded and primed. It was starting to look like a new playhouse, with the shutters ready to be rehung once the siding dried.

Madison pushed some stray strands of blond hair away from her forehead with the back of her hand, narrowly avoiding dripping paint on herself.

"I was still talking to that girl I had been with at boarding school—Hunter. We stayed friends after I left, and we were talking a lot, and I was with Elliot one day when she was sending me a bunch of texts. I went to the bathroom and accidentally left my phone unlocked, and he saw the texts. It wasn't even anything super explicit, but it was enough for him to get the picture."

I kept working while she talked, hoping it might take some of the pressure off if my eyes weren't on her. I knew how it could feel, baring a scary truth with someone else looked on. That unbearable weight of being known. Madison stopped for a moment, painting quietly for a few strokes.

"I came back out of the bathroom, and he confronted me about it immediately. He called me all kinds of names and slurs and even threw my phone into the wall and smashed the screen."

Another pause. The thick July air was heavy on my bare shoulders, the back of my neck slick with sweat. We'd been at it for a while and the heat was wearing on us both. But I stayed quiet. I let the hum of the woods fill up the silence.

"And then he grabbed me. First my arm, yanked me close to him. But when I tried to pull away, he grabbed my throat. I don't think I've ever been so scared. I don't know what I thought he was about to do, but at that point, he'd been a dick to me for weeks, and I had been watching it get progressively worse and not doing anything about it."

Her voice wavered. I stopped painting. I set my brush across the lid of my paint can and looked at her. She stared at the playhouse wall, paint dripping from her brush as she held it at her side.

"It was on me, really. I kept letting him get away with shit. Calling me names, calling me fat. Shaming me for every move I made. Of course he would think it was okay to fucking choke me. I let him think it would be. And honestly, had I just grown a spine right then and there and told him to eat shit when he said I was going to do whatever he told me to or else he'd out me, maybe he wouldn't have hurt that girl."

I took the paintbrush out of her hand and set it down. My hands went to her shoulders, and I made her face me with a gentle touch against her chin.

"Hey. Look at me. Listen to me. Nothing he did was your fault. He emotionally abused you until he knew you wouldn't fight back when it got worse. He manipulated you until he knew you'd blame yourself. He hurt that girl because he's an abuser, Madison. What happened to her—what happened to *you*—wasn't your fault. It was his."

Madison was looking at me, staring into my eyes like she was trying to commit what I was saying to memory. I gently squeezed her arms and let my hands drop down to hers, hooking my index fingers with hers.

"Maybe no one has ever called him out on his shit before, but that won't be the case for long. He's going to pay for what he did. For all of it. For that girl, for you. For everything he did before that and after."

I took a breath, letting go of Madison and picking up my brush.

"Some people have to learn their lessons the hard way," I added, getting back to painting, feeling her eyes still on me.

In my peripheral vision, I saw her wet her lips. I felt her step closer, moving behind me until her hands were against my hips, her chest pressing gently against my back. She ran her fingers along the top of my shorts, brushing the bit of exposed skin below the hem of my tank top. I felt her hot breath against the side of my neck as she moved her lips beside my ear, goose-bumps erupting over my bare arms, a shiver running through my limbs despite the thick heat.

"Did you teach Emma a lesson too, Tillie?"

My body went cold. My heart rattled out of its rhythm, and a rush of adrenaline quickened my pulse to a catastrophic speed. I worried my rib cage wouldn't be able to contain my thudding heart. She hadn't brought up Emma since the night I told her what happened. We'd fallen into a comfortable understanding that I didn't *want* to talk about it, much less even begin to explain myself. The same understanding I'd come to in my own head about keeping the details of Madison's time at Walden buried and silent.

The way she said it, though, felt more like a dare than a question. I felt her grip onto my hips and pull me back against her, her fingers sneaking under the waist of my shorts, one thumb working open the button so she could slip her hand down the front. I lost my breath as I tried to pull it into my lungs, a little whimper falling from my open mouth.

And that whimper came out sounding like—"*Yes.*"

I could never tell where her hunger for me was going to come from next. I was seeing, though, that it almost always started with a secret. She always wanted me the most when it was most apparent how deadly it would be to have me. We always wanted each other the most in the moments it was painfully clear that we were probably the worst thing for each other.

Madison had a way of showing me I was the villain in my own story while swearing I was the hero.

"That's how we'll do it," I said, later, sitting cross-legged on the dock beside Madison. The sun was starting to sink behind the trees on the other side of the lake.

"It was a text that set the whole thing off with him and you, yeah? So a text will be what fucks him over."

Madison popped a piece of watermelon in her mouth from the bowl of chopped fruit sitting between us.

"What do you mean?" She mumbled around a mouthful. "How?"

"I'm still working it out in my head, but...what if we cloned his number and sent a text to everyone we know that looks like him confessing to everything?"

Madison made a face and let out a laugh.

"Tillie. Clone his number? That isn't even a thing. Plus no one would believe it—even if we somehow had the tools to pull that off, they'd think he'd been hacked or had his phone stolen."

I opened my mouth to argue but quickly closed it with a sigh. She wasn't wrong. No one would buy that Elliot James had taken accountability for every bad thing he had ever done, especially since so many of them believed he really was innocent.

We sat in silence, both of us plucking pieces of fruit from the bowl, watching the light continue to darken across the lake. I listened to the water slosh gently against the bank behind us, trying to sort through all the bad ideas in my head, hoping to land on some feasible idea that would get Elliot where I wanted him.

"So, we steal his phone. He's always at the club. It shouldn't be that hard to lift his phone while he's swimming or up getting a drink or something. Then we use his phone to post something or send a text that'll incriminate him. We can send a text to your number, so it looks like he's talking to you about it. That's more believable than him sending some grand confession to his entire contact list. Although, he does have access to every single person at school's numbers. He said so to your brother."

While I spoke, rattling my way through the rough edges of an idea, Madison slowly chewed on a piece of pineapple, her eyes finally turning to look sideways at me. She unfolded her legs and let them drop over the edge of the dock, swinging loosely over the water.

"I mean," she started, swallowing and taking a moment to think. "It isn't a *terrible* idea. I guess even if he notices the text and deletes it, it'll still be on my phone, and the record of him sending it won't be erased."

I nodded, the pieces falling together in front of us, a full picture beginning to materialize.

"But Tillie," Madison went on, looking over at me fully. "Why do you care so much? Like, you don't *have* to do anything. Whether Elliot gets punished or not doesn't really affect you."

"You already know my answer to that," I pointed out. Madison reached over and touched my bent knee, tracing a little heart onto my skin with her fingertip.

"I know that part, but…there's gotta be more. Is this about what happened to that girl back in Philadelphia?"

With each mention, Emma had less and less of a whiplash on my insides. The sudden gut punch that usually accompanied her memory had dulled to a gentle thud, barely a rattle behind my ribs. I didn't know if that was because I was moving on, or if I had somehow transferred all that deeply rooted guilt and hurt to someone new. And the last thing I was going to do was question it. I felt too free to let Emma's ghost sneak back in through an open window. I didn't want to think of what would happen once Elliot's karma had been served, and my anger and pain would need a new shoreline to erode.

"I don't know," I finally said. "Maybe a little. But mostly? It's about the fact that this prick has gotten away with way more than anyone should. And I have no doubt he will keep doing shit like that once he gets to college."

Madison looked back out across the lake. I let her sit with my words. My thoughts settled back on the gentle movement of the water under the dock. The longer I listened to it, the more my thoughts wandered, until I was suddenly imagining the shape of a little girl moving toward the surface, eyes fixed open, body rocking with the push of the wind against the lake. I wondered about the man who had drowned Poppy and how they'd found his body. Had they sent divers down to cut the rope tied to the cinder block and let him float up? Had they left him there? Was he still down there somewhere, a pile of bones and a piece of cement?

"Jackson or Liam can help." Madison's voice brought me back

to the dock. "They both think Elliot is a piece of shit. We don't have to tell them much, just say that we need help distracting Elliot. And once he's not paying attention, we take his phone."

There was something contagious in our growing thirst for the vengeance we could enact. We were feeding off each other's anxious, furious energy, and the better, smarter, more honest part of myself was screaming from somewhere in the depths of my mind to stop now. The me from last summer, the one who hadn't yet watched Emma Charles disappear under the hard pull of an ocean current, was begging the me sitting there beside Madison to take a hard left turn and go somewhere else with all this rage. Anywhere else. I ignored her. Shoved her by the shoulders under the surface of my memory until her pleas were an echo. A whisper from underwater.

"Liam quit the club," I said, suddenly remembering what Gigi had said. "He doesn't work there anymore."

I wanted to add that I didn't think getting Liam involved in our schemes was a good idea to begin with, but I held that part back. I knew Madison would want to know why, but I wasn't sure I had an answer. When I thought of Liam, I thought of his tunnel to get out of Willow Creek and out from under his parents' thumb, and I felt oddly protective of that light at the end of it. After he'd picked me up from the pool deck and carried me to his car, gotten me dry and warm and pulled one of his own sweatshirts over my head, I couldn't see him as anything but good. The last thing I wanted, for some reason, was to sully him with whatever plans Madison and I were hatching.

"I'll get Jackson to help, then. He always says Elliot never tips."

I nodded. With our half-baked plan starting to come together, and with the way we had both so clearly decided to go through with it no matter how the pieces fell into place, I started to feel a strange comfort.

There was something like a blanket that had been pulled over us both, like we'd been restless sleepers, dreaming of all the wrongs done to us. And we both suddenly seemed to settle, Madison even letting out a soft hum, turning to look at me with a smile.

The sun had completely disappeared behind the trees, sending the lake into darkness. The moon had taken the sun's place, and its cool light set shadows on Madison's face, her silhouette on the dock enveloping mine as she pushed the fruit bowl out of the way. She draped her arm over my neck, and I lifted my hand to hold hers, turning toward her so her nose nearly touching mine. Her smile brightened.

Still, there was a darkness in it. In her smile, in her eyes, in the needy, hungry way we were latching on to one another more and more, as if a second without our hands on each other was like hours without a full breath in. The only person I had ever felt that kind of need for before was back in Philadelphia, forgetting I existed. A vital organ, cut out of me without anesthetic, my body having to learn to function without it.

And then came Madison, wearing a grin and holding a scalpel, promising to make it all better.

Chapter Fourteen

It took another week for everything to fall into place.

We had to make it happen before school started the first week of August. Without the long, free summer days, we knew we'd had fewer chances to catch Elliot at the club. Temple classes started at the end of August, and most of the Temple kids in Willow Creek left a week early for orientation, according to Madison. Her older brother Remi split his time between Philly and Willow Creek all summer, freely coming and going, showing up unannounced at their house whenever he needed cash or to steal a few bottles from their parents' wine cellar. But she looked forward to the day he'd go back to Philly and stay there until Thanksgiving, or so she'd always angrily mumble whenever we went to her house and his car was in the driveway.

I didn't have siblings, so I never questioned her disdain for

Remi. I knew it was something I probably wouldn't ever fully get. But I had a feeling that Remi's friendship with Elliot had something to do with Madison wanting to snap his branch off the family tree.

I let Madison deal with anything involving going to the club. Going there still felt a little like returning to the scene of a crime. But the day before we were hoping to execute our plan, Madison drove us over to the club, insisting she had to make a stop.

"Couldn't you have done this before coming to pick me up?" I argued from her passenger seat as she hung a left off the parkway, taking the short, winding road to the club.

"Tillie. I know you think everyone wants to burn you at the stake or something, but I can promise you—people don't care. They've all forgotten and moved on. I know it sounds shitty, but these people are shitty, so that's how it goes."

I didn't have to convince myself she was right. I knew she was. The rich people in Willow Creek would only milk the accidental death of some little kid for as long as it did something for them. Or until another scandal consumed their attention, and I had heard that one of the club wives had just caught her very high-profile, very wealthy husband with another man—so there was little doubt that all their attention had shifted from Lottie's death.

"Either way," I said, crossing my arms and sinking farther into my seat, "I'm staying in the car."

Madison let out a laugh as she pulled into the front lot, swinging the BMW into a spot near the entrance.

"Okay, you do that, pouty baby."

She left the engine running, and I watched her walk to the front entrance, her hand raising in a wave to a group of people leaving as she went inside. I sighed and wished I could disappear, wanting nothing less than to be seen and, even less, to have to talk to anyone.

But before I could decide whether I wanted to lay my seat all the way back and get out of view, a tap on the passenger window made my pulse jump, my hand pressing to the center of my chest.

Liam was standing outside the window, a smile coming to his face when my eyes met his. A string of curse words rattled its way through my head as I pushed the button to lower the window.

"Tillie," he said, resting his hand against the car and leaning in a little. "I was wondering if I'd see you again before I left for school."

I pressed my lips into a tight, thin smile.

"I was hoping if you saw me, it wouldn't have to be *here*."

Both of us glanced in unison at the club entrance, then looked back to each other.

"I asked Gigi about you. She said you were doing okay. But I'm glad I get to find that out for myself, now."

I lifted my shoulders in a shrug and let them fall again heavily.

"Doing 'okay' is all relative, I guess." I suddenly wished I could silence the whiny, angsty voice that was the only way I could communicate when someone brought up what happened to Lottie.

"I mean, I doubt anyone would expect you to be in tip-top shape," Liam said, his voice softening.

I gave him a sad smile.

"You're here with Madison, huh?" He added, nodding toward the empty driver's seat. I looked over at Madison's ivory velvet scrunchie around the gear shift.

"Uh…" I started, then shrugged, knowing there was no point in playing it off. "Yeah. She…had to run in for something. We're just, you know, hanging out."

Shut up, shut up, shut up—the voice in my head was screaming. *You fucking idiot, stop while you're ahead.*

"Hm," Liam hummed, and I felt panic rise into my chest, that quiet hum sounding too all-knowing for my comfort.

"Hm what?"

"Oh, I wouldn't have pegged you two as being friends," he went on, standing up a little straighter. "But I guess that would explain why her A-team has been without a leader for a few weeks. Or so I noticed before I quit taking shifts."

I looked toward the club entrance, thinking of Madison's little pride of lionesses inside by the pool, wearing their designer swimsuits with their bodies draped over the chaise longues under a cabana, staring disinterestedly into their phones. Without their queen, they were likely a disjointed, dissolving kingdom, a band of duchesses with no one to impress. I hadn't thought of them much in the weeks since I'd last seen them at the club. Some part of me wanted to be a ghost in the corner when they collectively realized the only subject their queen wanted to rule over was me.

But, if Liam was noticing, they probably were too.

"Yeah, we don't hang out constantly, so I don't why she hasn't been coming here," I lied, and I knew it was painfully obvious that I was.

Liam chuckled and leaned his hand on the car again, ducking in closer to the window.

"Tillie," he said, his voice low. "It's okay. I'm not a Trojan horse. I know it might seem like I'm one of them, but believe me when I tell you, the second I get outta this town, I'm making it my mission to surround myself with people the opposite of them."

I watched him while he spoke, saw the way his eyes looked back at the club after he fell quiet again, a strange longing on his face.

"I know you aren't like them," I said. "And neither is she."

I nodded toward the empty driver's seat.

Liam rested his forearms in the window, close enough so that I could see the gentleness in his face, the genuine concern and care written into the lines on his forehead.

"I haven't always thought the best of Madison Frank," he admitted, softly. "But ever since everything happened with Elliot James, I've always wondered how much of that shit was really her choice. I know sometimes you do shit you don't mean or don't want to do because it'll mean the difference between fitting in and falling out—and the last thing you wanna do in a town like this is to fall out."

"I keep hearing that," I said, feeling that familiar rush of angry heat in my chest at the mere mention of Elliot James. "Is this town some kind of black hole, or something?"

"You could say that," he sighed. "But really it's just a small town full of people so intent on holding on to the status quo that they punish outliers. There's nothing special about Willow Creek. There are a million Willow Creeks. We're simply stuck in this one."

"Well, you aren't stuck for much longer," I reminded him, giving his arm on the door a little nudge.

Liam smiled.

"I guess I should make sure I return your sweatshirt before you go, huh?"

He shook his head. "Nah. You're good. Keep it."

I wasn't sure I wanted to keep that tangible reminder of a tragedy. But still, the idea of keeping it was oddly comforting.

I gave him a nod, and he stepped back from the window.

"Try and stay outta trouble, huh, Tillie Gray?"

I gave Liam a playful salute, and he turned, heading for his car parked the far side of the lot. My eyes stayed on him, so Madison's sudden reappearance caught me off guard as she opened the driver's-side door.

"Shocked to see Liam here," she noted, buckling her seat belt. "I figured he'd disappear the moment he quit."

I shrugged and put my sunglasses back on.

"I get the feeling the webs spun around here are a little difficult to untangle."

"You're not wrong."

I looked back over at Madison, watching her collect herself before pressing on the brake and putting the BMW in reverse.

"So what was this little stop all about?" I asked, picking Madison's phone from one of the cupholders to scroll through her music.

"I was checking to see if Elliot still had his usual Saturday-morning golf round on the books for tomorrow," she said, reversing out of the parking spot and pressing on the gas pedal to whip us toward the parkway again.

"And?"

She threw me a smirk, hanging a left onto the main road toward her house.

"He does. And after he plays, he always has lunch at the club restaurant with his dad and whatever other bigwig rich dudes are in town for the weekend. It's always a see-and-be-seen affair on Saturdays there. They never miss it. Their tee time is at eight, and they'll be in the restaurant by twelve-thirty."

I nodded and selected a song to play, dropping Madison's phone back into the center console. She turned up the volume. An old Labrinth song filled the space inside the car, our rolled-down windows letting the warm late July day push through our hair.

There was something that felt final about that drive away from the club, like a puzzle piece that had revealed the whole picture. We were so ready to line up the nails and beat them into the lid of Elliot's coffin that we hardly noticed we were hammering from the inside.

Chapter Fifteen

If my heart had been thudding any harder, I was sure it would have broken through my rib cage and tumbled onto the floor. I could feel my pulse in my ears, drowning out the hum of voices and laughter coming from the club's dining room, my back pressed hard to the wall. I felt like I was trespassing, being at the club again. As I peeked around the corner, I could see straight through to the wall of glass along the back that looked out to the pool deck. I could just make out Gigi, perched up in the guard stand, blowing her whistle at a kid sprinting toward the snack bar.

I pulled back behind the wall again and tried to focus. I checked my phone—12:33. Madison said she would text me when she saw Elliot and his dad get seated in the dining room. She'd set up her stakeout at the bar, attempting to be incognito with her blond hair tucked into a neat bun, a nondescript black sundress on, grazing idly on a salad. I slid down the wall a bit, so I could look around the other side, where I could see Madison at the bar, eating and looking at her phone. Even from my position, I could see she had the front-facing camera on, using it to look behind herself at the dining room.

I couldn't see farther in. I had no way of knowing when Elliot had arrived until Madison told me, unless I went into the dining room myself, a move I knew would give us away too easily. Not only had I not shown my face at the club since the accident, but Elliot knew Madison and I had been hanging out, and he knew enough to put the pieces together and get suspicious.

My phone buzzed in my hand.

incoming.

I peeked back into the dining room, catching a glimpse of Elliot and a man I assumed was his dad—a tall, broad, man with Elliot's same razor-sharp angles and with salt-and-pepper hair—coming inside from the pro shop, following a hostess to a table. They were seated right in the middle of the dining room, and I cursed under my breath, already panicking about how we were going to pull this off without being noticed.

Another text came in: wait for drinks.

I craned my neck to see Madison, and she shot me a look from the bar, making me realize how insane and conspicuous

I probably looked right then, half my torso leaned into the dining room.

I stepped to the other dining room entrance, hoping to get a better view. As I tried to quietly move through the club lobby, my shoulder collided with a body, sending me back a step. My hip bumped the corner of a decorative end table, knocking a small brochure stand onto the floor with a loud clatter.

"Oh shit—"

"Tillie?"

I looked up from frantically corralling the loose brochures, feeling like a deer in headlights. Half the lobby and some of the people in the dining room looked over at me. Standing above me was Lindy, another lifeguard at the club. A smile cut through the confused look on her face.

"Oh, hey, Lindy."

"I haven't seen you since—" she stopped abruptly, and I watched her cheeks darken before she could collect herself. "I haven't seen you in a while."

I stood, holding a messy stack of brochures, wishing I could evaporate.

"Um, yeah. I just…you know. I haven't really come around."

I could feel eyes on me. I glanced over and saw Madison at the bar, her eyes widening, lips mouthing *what the fuck*.

"Yeah…When you stopped showing up on the schedule, I figured as much."

Lindy put on an awkward smile. I mirrored it back, holding the brochures like I'd shown up at the club specifically for those.

Lindy was a college kid, home from some school up in New York. That was about all I knew of her, aside from the way her laugh could echo across the entire pool deck, and the way Jackson's eyes followed the gentle sway of her full hips as she walked. We'd hardly interacted during my brief tenure as a guard, but here she was, looking at me like I was a long-lost friend.

I dropped the brochures in a pile on the table I'd knocked into, carefully setting the plastic display stand on top.

"Actually," I said, pausing to picked up a stray brochure from the floor and tossing it onto the table, "I have to go, Lindy. So sorry. So nice to see you though."

"Um, yeah, you too."

I was already hurrying away, taking quick strides past the entrance to the dining room, disappearing from Madison's— and everyone else's—view. Once I was around the corner, I flattened my back against the wall, letting out a few quick, anxious breaths. I was right near one of the doors to the pool deck, and I tried to recalculate on the fly, mapping out an inconspicuous route back to the dining room in my head. My phone buzzed in my hand, three times in fast succession.

TILLIE

where did u go?????

GET BACK 2 DINING RM NOW

I took in a deep breath. Every single thing that could go wrong seemed to be doing exactly that. I wanted to grab

Madison and leave the club before either of us could any deeper into this.

But the thought of Elliot James, laughing over Arnold Palmers with his rich dad, so completely and perpetually unscathed by any consequences of any of his actions, spurred my anger. And I knew I had to do whatever I could to make sure his winning streak came to an abrupt, deserved end.

I headed out the side door that led to the pool deck. If I followed the sidewalk alongside the deck, I could slip into the side door on the other end of the dining room by the pro shop without being obvious. I kept my pace steady, making sure not to walk too fast or too slow, smiling at people who passed me. Once there was no one coming, I broke into a jog, ducking behind the drink stand at the far end of the deck, where the golfers could grab beers before they hit the course. Behind the drink stand was the door into the pro shop, and I carefully pulled it open and ventured inside, gratefully finding myself in the back with no one in the immediate vicinity.

I quickly scanned the room, looking for any familiar faces that may notice me and want to strike up conversation, and thankfully saw no one I knew. I stepped through the shop and toward the entrance of the restaurant, narrowly dodging the eye of a hostess as I moved into the room. I cut across the back wall where the servers kept the drink refill pitchers and settled in the far corner, where I could see both Elliot at his table and Madison on the other side of the room at the bar.

Madison's eyes found me, and she gave me a small nod. I

watched her, slowly sinking down onto a bench near the waiting area, hoping I'd be less noticeable. I saw Madison nod to someone else, and realized it was to Jackson, who at the opposite end of the bar. He flashed her a smirk and picked up a small tray of water glasses, carrying them toward Elliot's table. Just as he made it to their table and started to unload the glasses, he feigned a sudden stumble, knocking one of the glasses over and onto Elliot.

From halfway across the room, I could hear Elliot's deep voice thunder through the space.

"Christ, watch what you're doing!"

"I'm sorry," Jackson said, his voice dripping in insincerity. "Can I get you a towel?"

"No, I can handle it." Elliot snapped, pushing back from the table. He shot Jackson a glare as he stomped off in the direction of the restrooms in the lobby.

I eyed the table. Elliot's cell phone was facedown by his bread plate. I looked to Madison. She signaled for me to wait.

Jackson stepped closer to Elliot's father, keeping his attention as he continued to apologize for the spill. This was what she'd wanted me to wait for.

I sucked in a deep breath and got up, weaving my way through the room, hips dodging tables and chair backs. My heart was pounding in my ears as I approached Elliot's table. I went to move past Jackson, making a subtle show of saying excuse me and brushing behind him, my hand dropping to the table to swipe Elliot's phone, quickly dropping it into the pocket of my shorts.

My entire body shifted into autopilot, guiding me out of the dining room. I hardly noticed where I was going until Madison fell into step beside me. The two of us walked together through the lobby and down a side hallway that would take us to the side lot where we'd parked her car.

We'd made it out the side door and were almost to the lot when we heard a voice behind us.

"You're kidding, right?"

The voice felt like barbed wire catching both of our necks. We stopped in our tracks. We looked at each other before turning toward the source, my stomach dropping toward my knees.

Elliot stepped toward us. Instinctively, like it was muscle memory, I took one protective sidestep in front of Madison. Elliot only chuckled.

"You two didn't think you'd get away with that for real, did you?"

We stayed silent. He took another step closer.

"I clocked both of you the second we sat down. You think I didn't know you'd be trying to come after me?"

"Eat a dick, Elliot." Madison snapped from behind me. I reached one hand back and grabbed her wrist, squeezing hard to hush her.

"We don't even know what you're talking about," I said, my voice narrowly avoiding an audible crack.

He let out another laugh, this one edged with annoyance.

"Just give it to me before you make yourselves look any more like fucking idiots."

Madison and I both stayed silent, but I could feel her breaths on my shoulder, hot and quick. The anger was radiating off her in waves. I knew at any moment, she'd break, and I'd be wrestling her off him.

After another beat where none of us spoke, Elliot threw his hands up.

"All right, fine."

He lifted his arm, showing us the smart watch on his wrist, and I immediately knew we were fucked. I hadn't checked his phone as we'd walked out make sure it was silent or even to see if I could put it on airplane mode. I'd been so anxious to get out of there that I hadn't thought that far ahead.

With a tap of a button on his watch, Elliot's phone started vibrating and alarming in my back pocket.

Madison and I stood frozen. I closed my eyes for a second, as if I could somehow will us to be somewhere, anywhere else.

Frustrated by our inaction, Elliot glared at us and stepped to me, barely inches between our bodies. I returned his glare, my grip on Madison's wrist tightening, hoping she could somehow hear me internally screaming *don't fucking do it*.

Elliot reached around my body and slipped his fingers into my back pocket. My entire body was full of pins and needles, every limb suddenly heavy and tense, my brain trying to detach, so I wouldn't have to perceive what was happening. I felt his hand purposefully rub against my backside as he pulled his phone from my pocket.

I could feel my expression set into anger as I consciously fought off the urge to spit directly in his face.

He leaned down, getting his face closer to mine. I felt Madison tense behind me, and I used my grip on her to push her back.

"I know it was you two fucking sluts who keyed my car," he said, voice low. "You're gonna wish you'd never fucked with me." His eyes went to me again. "Both of you."

Finally he put space between our bodies again. A smirk curled onto his lips that sent my stomach into a tight knot.

"It's been a pleasure, as always, Maddie," he added with a little chuckle, before turning and walking back into the club, shutting the door behind him.

Chapter Sixteen

In the days after our run-in with Elliot at the club, I found myself weighed down in my bed again, trapped somewhere between furious and resigned. I still had so much anger shored up inside me, all of it a fire I could only extinguish by punishing Elliot James. But the longer I laid in my bed, the more time I had to be alone inside my own head, wandering the halls of my thoughts, running into dead ends each time I wondered why I wanted Elliot to be punished so badly.

There was the obvious reason—he deserved it. He had gotten away with something so egregious, so disgusting, that being held accountable was the absolute bare minimum of what could and should happen to him. He had hurt Madison, physically and emotionally, had backed her into so many corners that the only thing she could think to do was fight her way out of them with sharp words and cruelty, even when it was misdirected. I blamed him for the things Madison had done wrong in the wake of him, convinced that she had only been twisted into an unfamiliar version of herself by his hands.

But, if I was honest with myself, if Elliot's darkness deserved punishment, didn't mine?

Laying on my back in my bed, listening to the quiet hum of the small fan on my night table, counting the glowing lights on the strings hung across my ceiling, I tried to decide if I had been punished enough. The bad thing I'd done had been in the name of keeping the one good thing I had, and I'd lost that good thing. Then, Lottie Southerland died on my watch. Drowned in four feet of water barely a few yards from where I'd sat, fixated on Elliot James.

Had I not paid for what I'd done? Had I not suffered enough to level the scales? Who got to decide that?

I rolled over to sit up, grabbing my phone from the night table. The last text I'd gotten was from Madison, telling me she'd be over to get me after my mom went to work. We'd been avoiding our parents, only leaving our rooms to be with each other once all of our coasts were clear. We'd both grown tired of explaining ourselves, answering prying questions about why we were only ever with one another, not-so-subtle inquiries about our other friends and how they were doing. We *wanted* to be alone together. Alone together where the world revolved around only us, and where all our pain and need and desperation didn't have to feel self-serving and useless.

When I was alone without her, I was left to stray into rooms and hallways in my mind that I had tried to wall up. Alone without her, all the places in my memory that I had tried to erase like a cartographer redrawing a map, reappeared, freshly painted red doors waiting to be opened. Thinking of her led me down the road to thinking of Greer, the last pair of arms I had laid comfortably within, feeling like I'd found a home, just for someone to burn it to the ground.

Loving someone as wholly and intensely as I loved Greer had unlocked something inside me that I had since tried to lock back up, but that Madison was steadily unlocking again, every touch another click in the combination.

I opened Instagram and scrolled through my feed to pass a few more long moments while waiting for Madison. I double tapped a few photos from friends back in Philly and one from Gigi working behind the counter at her parents' shop. I scrolled and scrolled, waiting for Greer to pop up, my connection to her limited to photos, always grinning with some new friend or another. Nothing from her appeared on my feed, so I typed in her username. When I hit the search button, it returned with a simple phrase: *No results found*.

My pulse picked up. My throat tightened, heat rising from my chest into my neck. I erased and retyped it. The same result. I went back to my profile and clicked *Following*, and searched for her name there.

Nothing.

I quickly toggled over to my burner account and looked from there. Nothing.

My breaths starting to come in harsh, quick huffs, I closed Instagram and opened my browser, typing *greer holland instagram* and her username into the search bar. The first result was the link to her Instagram profile, clearly still active. When I opened the link in my browser, it showed me a preview of her profile, the most recent few posts and a link to log in or sign up for Instagram to see more. I tapped the button to open her profile in Instagram, and when the app opened, I was met with another blank search screen. *No results found.*

Greer had blocked me.

Facebook, Snapchat, and even the old Tumblr we'd shared—blocked, blocked, deleted.

I dropped my phone on my bed and slid into the corner where my mattress met the wall, pulling my knees to my chest. Even if Greer and I hadn't actually spoken in months, I'd still held on to that connection like a last lifeline. Some part of me had been convinced that she would eventually come back, that I'd see her name appear on my phone, that I'd go down to Philly to be with her on weekends, and we'd pick up where we left off. Even with Madison filling up so many of my waking hours, I still spent too much time wishing for Greer, for what we'd had before. Before Stone Harbor. Before Emma had chosen Greer as her prey and hunted her for sport with no other reason than to ruin me.

As I sat there running everything through my head, something shifted. That connection, that last tenuous grip I'd had on the Before, was suddenly gone. Now there was only the After. Now there was only Madison, and my desire to do everything in my power to keep her...to protect what we were building. And whatever last bit of restraint I had to keep me from acting on all the fury that was seated in my chest—it was gone.

If Greer wanted to erase me, I could erase her right back.

My phone lit up with a notification and I watched it for a second before willing myself to move out of the corner and pick it up.

A text message from an unknown number.

you're gonna pay bitch.

A photo popped up under the text, sending my heart into my throat. It was a picture of my house.

"Tillie? I'm heading out to work—"

I leapt out of bed, throwing my bedroom door open in time to catch my mom standing there, looking surprised to see me.

"Wait, just hold on."

I pushed past her and down the hallway, running to the front door. I opened it and stepped outside in my bare feet, walking onto the front lawn in my pajamas, scanning the street. I didn't see anything—no unfamiliar cars, no shadows ducking behind a neighbor's house, not even an out-of-place garbage bin at the end of a driveway.

"Til, what's wrong?"

I gave the street one more look before turning to my mom. I swallowed the thick lump of fear that had gathered in my throat, shaking my head.

"Nothing, nothing's wrong."

I walked back to the door and met her there, kissing her cheek.

"Have a good shift."

She still looked bewildered, eyeing me like I was speaking gibberish. She finally nodded and walked to her car, and I watched her get in and back out of the driveway, waving as she drove away. I hurried back inside and shut the door, locking the handle and deadbolt.

I knew exactly who had sent the text, but I stood there, working to convince myself that he wasn't a real threat, that he was just trying to scare me in retaliation for scheming to expose him, or for the word Madison had keyed into the side of his car.

Madison.

Before I could run for my phone to call her, a hard knock at the front door nearly sent me into cardiac arrest. I pressed close and looked through the peephole, letting out a relieved breath to see Madison standing there. I unlocked and opened the door, and she quickly stepped inside, turning and showing me her phone screen.

"He's fucking with me."

She had a text on her screen from an unknown number with

the same message that had been sent to me. But instead of a photo of her house, there was a photo of her getting into her car. She was wearing the same clothes in the photo as she was while she stood there in front of me, so I knew the photo had been from today.

"Where was—"

"I was getting in the car after going to my mom's work. I don't know how he could have even known I was there unless he's been stalking me."

I took in a slow, deep breath, trying to calm my still-racing pulse. I shook my head a little, the pieces of this particular puzzle not coming together in my head the way I needed them to.

"It doesn't make any sense," I said. I beckoned Madison to follow me down the hall to my bedroom. I showed her the text and photo I'd gotten, and even in the low light of my room, I could see the color leave her face.

"Why's he doing this?" I pushed. "What's in it for him? He beat us. Our plan to screw him over didn't work. So why come after us?"

Madison put her phone into her back pocket and chewed her lip, pacing in my small bedroom.

"You don't know Elliot. He doesn't need some big reason. You just need to look at him wrong for him to want to destroy you. He knows I keyed his car, and he knows you were there, and he knows we tried to steal his phone. I'm sure he knows why we tried to do that."

She stopped pacing and looked at me.

"He's not going to stop. He's not only trying to scare us. He's going to do something; I just don't know what yet."

"He's leaving for school soon, though, right? So maybe he is fucking with us and soon he'll give up and be gone."

Madison shook her head, taking my shoulders in her hands, making me look at her.

"Tillie," she said, an edge of fear in her voice that I didn't recognize. "He won't give up."

From the way she was looking at me, and from the way her grip on my shoulders tightened, I knew she meant it. She knew more about Elliott James and what set him off better than anyone. In my head, I saw his hand around her throat, her smashed cell phone at her feet, his rage reflected in her wide eyes. She was right.

He wasn't going to give up until one or both of us was ruined.

Chapter Seventeen

The first week in August, school started.

Back in Philly, classes rarely began before September, but in Willow Creek the high school started earlier to allow for a Welcome Back Week, potential winter snow days, and the school year ending in early June. Since moving to Willow Creek, I'd been panicked about starting school somewhere new. Everything I'd learned about Willow Creek High had made it sound like an inner circle of hell, where literally everyone was discovering your flaws and secrets to destroy you.

With the added shadow of Elliot James, the impending first day felt like a minor speed bump before a cliff.

The morning of the first day, Mom was waiting for me in the kitchen when I dragged myself down the hall, still half asleep and already texting Madison, asking her when she'd be there to pick me up. I had been a little surprised when she'd offered to drive me, part of me assuming we were going to keep our relationship low-key and out of sight to spare us whatever wrath we might face if people saw us together. But Madison had only shrugged when I'd said as much.

"You're going to be the new kid. And I'll be the nice kid who decided to show you the ropes. It doesn't have to be more complicated than that."

Her words stung. I knew Madison was nowhere close to being who she was openly, but to hear her detail how she was going to make us small enough to fold and hide away was still a blow to the gut.

"Well, if it isn't my morning sunshine," my mom teased, chuckling at the sight of my tired eyes and careless bun.

"You look like you are so, so ready to face this day, my little bean."

I wrinkled my nose and dropped my backpack, looking for something in the kitchen to eat, figuring Madison would have coffees for us like always. That must be why she hadn't texted me back yet.

I zipped an apple into my backpack for later and went to the front window, checking for Madison's car. The street was empty other than a neighbor leaving for work. I checked my phone again and sent another text, adding it to the three others I'd already sent that morning.

are u coming???

"Til, you want me to drive you, baby? I can drive you. You don't wanna be late, yeah?" My mom watched me from the kitchen doorway, sipping her coffee, concern starting to bring her eyebrows together.

I stared out the front window, willing Madison's car to appear in the driveway. Another long moment passed, and I could hear my mom behind me, pulling on a sweater and picking up her keys.

She gave my arm a gentle squeeze.

"C'mon, maybe she overslept. You can text her again when you get there."

I looked at her, chewing my bottom lip, my eyes straying right back to the window, some hope still lingering. But I nodded. Even if Madison had overslept, or the Starbucks line was long, my mom wasn't going to let me be late first day at a new school. This was another chapter in our fresh start, one she had so carefully and hopefully written for us. I didn't want to let her down.

In the passenger seat of my mom's RAV4, I sent another text.

went with mom, see you there

No response had chimed through by the time I was standing on the curb outside the school, watching my mom disappear through the drop-off line.

Willow Creek High stood in front of me, looming at the end of the walkway, with students milling through the sets of double doors at the entrance. I looked around the student parking lot, eyeing every row for Madison's BMW, but it wasn't there. Some part of me felt mildly relieved that she hadn't come without me, but more of me was twisted and tense, wondering why she hadn't shown up yet.

Inside everyone was filtering through a series of check-in tables, getting their schedules, and heading off to find their homerooms. When I made it to the front of the table, a young-looking woman with smooth brown skin and tight black curls grinned up at me.

"Good morning, hi! Last name?"

"Good morning—uhh—Gray?"

She flipped through a file folder labeled with the letter G and hummed to herself, eventually pulling a sheet of paper from the thin stack.

"Tillie Gray?"

"That's me."

"Ahh, welcome to Willow Creek, Tillie! It says you're a transfer." She tapped a spot on the paper up near where my name was printed. "Your homeroom is with Ms. Clayton in the science hallway, so that's around this corner here." She pointed to her left, where some students were turning down a hallway, the wall painted with beakers, planets, and scattered letters from the periodic table. "Room 14."

I nodded and gave her a tight-lipped smile, taking my schedule from her. I was on edge, and I was hesitant to believe her kindness was even real, waiting for the other shoe to drop.

Ms. Clayton's room was a few doors into the science hallway, and I found my way inside, grabbing a seat at a table in the back row. With kids filing in and talking loudly, I tugged my phone out of my pocket and held it under the table, checking for anything from Madison.

But there was nothing. No responses, no missed calls. Only a push notification from my device management that said my screen time had increased from the day before. I sighed and shut my phone off, tucking it back into my pocket, just in time for the second bell to ring.

Two of Madison's friends slipped through the doorway as the bell rang—Sienna and Jules. They looked as beautiful as they had at the pool, but today instead of designer swimsuits, they'd donned almost matching pairs of black jeans and cropped short-sleeve button-ups. I watched them from the back of the room, half praying they didn't notice me. But the moment their eyes caught mine, I saw them lean in and whisper to one another, smirking as they spoke and ignoring Ms. Clayton as she stepped in front of the room and called for everyone to take a seat and stop talking.

"Sienna, Jules, I know without a doubt that whatever it is, it can wait."

The girls both huffed and sat back in their chairs, quieting and folding their arms.

"Good morning and welcome back, seniors! Your final year. Let's make it a good one, all right? Starting with today—Mr. Landry, I know you heard me say to put your phones away."

My eyes kept flicking to the classroom door, half expecting Madison to burst in. I didn't know what homeroom she had, but I was willing it to be this one, desperate for her to show up.

"We have a new student joining our senior class this year," Ms. Clayton said from the front of the room. "Tillie? Tillie Gray?"

Like a scene from a bad movie, everyone in the room turned in their seats to look at me. I froze, heat rising into my neck, my throat suddenly tight as I realized the exact thing I *hadn't* wanted to happen was happening.

"Did you want to say anything about yourself, Tillie?"

Ms. Clayton lifted her eyebrows at me. Every eye in the room was now trained on my slowly reddening face. I wiped my sweaty palms on the knees of my jeans.

"No, no, that's okay," I managed to mumble, shaking my head, earning a confused look from my homeroom teacher.

"All right then...well, welcome, Tillie. Now, everyone, you'll meet here for homeroom on Monday mornings..."

Her voice faded into background noise as my mind tried to remember the last things Madison had texted.

She was going to come by and pick me up before school.

She had sent a row of purple hearts in our text conversation last night before I fell asleep.

But this morning, radio silence.

I dropped back into my body when the bell rang, and I jumped up to leave the room, not even glancing at my schedule to know where I was headed next. I just hurried out of the room and back into the science hallway, retracing my steps toward the front entryway. The check-in table was still set up but unstaffed, and all the folders had been taken away. I couldn't check to see if Madison's schedule had been picked up yet. I stood there in front of the entrance to the office, pulling my phone back out of my pocket. Each time I did, I was hoping I to see Madison's string of hurried apologies—*sry, slept late! sry, coffee before anything!*—but nothing was there.

As I pulled my phone out this time, something *did* appear on my screen. A message sent from a number I didn't recognize but with my name listed as the sender, like it had come from my phone.

I unlocked my phone, and the message window opened.

TILLIE GRAY KILLED MADISON FRANK.

Every last bit of air was sucked out of the building, the hallway suddenly a black hole with too much gravity, paralyzing me, cementing my shoes to the floor.

And then everyone else's phones started chiming with new messages. It only took a few gasps and shouts for me to realize that they were getting the same message I had.

I watched the message make its way around the crowded hallway, everyone looking from their phones and then to those around them.

When the picture came next, I felt the floor tip upward. I was standing on the ceiling, looking down at myself as I stared at the photo on my screen of Madison's body, her eyes closed and blood dripping from the corner of her mouth. Her limbs were splayed like a doll that had been dropped. A smear of red was streaked through a chunk of her blond hair.

And while I stood on the ceiling, watching every phone in the hallway light up with the picture of Madison's body, I saw black water start to seep in from under the front doors.

Chapter Eighteen

On one of the afternoons we spent at the playhouse, Madison had asked me if I believed in ghosts.

We were sanding down the shutters after clumsily repairing the broken slats.

She'd pushed her hair back from her face, her cheek smeared with white dust. I gave her a shrug, a dull ache still thudding in my head while we worked.

"I'm not sure," I lied. I knew ghosts were real. A few of them followed me everywhere, hovering in the proverbial corner of every space I occupied.

"Why?" I asked her, shifting the focus off me.

"I don't know," she started, getting back to sanding. "I just think there's something about this place. And, you know, it's a cemetery. But there's something about this particular plot of earth. This house. The stones here. I feel like there are still some people here, lingering. Maybe trapped."

I sat back on my heels, dropping my sandpaper square, and wiping my hands on my T-shirt.

"Is that why you like us fixing this place up?" I asked, wetting my lips, and tasting sweat on them. "You think maybe when we do, she won't be trapped here anymore?"

"Or," Madison started, "I think maybe when we finish this, she'll be happy here."

I knew then that Madison's fascination with Poppy Holloway wasn't the simple fixation of a teenage girl desperate to be noticed. Madison *was* Poppy—a victim of circumstance, ready to settle for being trapped so long as she could be trapped in peace.

I was thinking about that day at the playhouse as I sat in the principal's office, dissociating from what was happening around me. I could hear my name being called, could hear people trying to talk to me, but my mind was somewhere else, in that quiet corner on the far side of Hidden Lake, watching Madison sand down the shutters of a dead girl's playhouse.

"Tillie."

I finally lifted my eyes from the spot I'd been fixed on, finding the source of the voice. It was Ms. Vaughn, the principal, whose face I hadn't ever laid eyes on before she'd found me in the hallway, flanked on either side by a school resource officer. She had a short-cropped haircut and soft features, but I could tell she was trying to soften them an attempt to put me at ease. It wasn't working. Every time I blinked, I saw the picture of Madison behind my eyes, her splayed-out body, the smear of red in her hair.

"Tillie, we know the message didn't come from your phone."

This time, it was another voice that chimed in. A detective, an older woman with dark hair tied back in a low ponytail. Detective Morales? I couldn't remember how she'd introduced herself. She had a slight accent, and my brain focused instead on trying to place it. Puerto Rican, maybe?

"The message came from a text app. It's an untraceable number. There isn't much information we can glean from it. But maybe you know someone who might have wanted to hurt Madison Frank? Or someone who wanted to hurt you?"

I lifted my eyes to the detective's. She stopped talking, like she was willing me to fill the empty space with an easy answer. And I knew I had one. But I didn't want to give it to her when I was certain it wouldn't be believed. I knew the moment I gave Elliot's name to the cops, they'd think I was bullshitting them, handing them the name of someone who Madison had so vehemently defended. Someone who had been wrongfully accused before, or so everyone thought. Who would I be to them but another teenage girl, lying for attention?

I shook my head.

"I don't know who did this. I don't know where she is."

Even in the precarious situation I'd found myself in, I still wasn't going to spill Madison's secrets, of which I was one. Everything she'd done, she'd done to protect herself. She had her secrets, and I had mine. We kept them dutifully, indebted to each other for our simple understanding to stay quiet.

Principal Vaughn and Detective Morales both sighed, almost in perfect unison. A collective hum of disappointment in me. I wasn't offering them anything. All I wanted was to get out of that room and find Madison. I was still so certain she was alive, that the photo was either exaggerated or faked to hurt me. I knew Elliot wasn't going to make it that simple. There was more. This was just his first act. What fun would it be for him to kill Madison and not watch me find out about it in real time? I didn't know much about him, but I knew he was the kind of person who thrived on the power he held over others. He would keep Madison under his thumb for as long as he could.

I had to get out of here so I could figure out his next move. I stared at my phone, sitting on Vaughn's desk in between us, silent and blank. I wanted to grab it and run out, but I knew I wouldn't make it far. The resource officer, his hand still perched on his holstered gun, was hovering outside the office door.

"Madison's mother reported her missing a little while ago," the detective said. "Did you speak to her at all last night or today?"

I knew Madison had still been safe before I'd gone to bed, and I was suddenly trying to map out her usual steps, thinking of where she might have gone last night. Or maybe it wasn't last night at all. Maybe it was this morning, as she was leaving to pick me up for school. Or, as she was going to pick up coffee for us. He knew her routine well enough, and we both knew he'd been following her.

"I, uh…" I shook my head, trying to collect my racing thoughts long enough to spit out something coherent for them to run with. "Yeah I, um, she texted me last night, before I went to bed, but that was it."

Vaughn and Morales exchanged glances. They were both clearly tiring of my rudderless responses. Before either of them could ask me anything else, the office door swung open, and my mom appeared, windswept and flushed in her scrubs.

"Tillie, oh my God."

I stood and easily fell into her tight hold, the ache in my chest deepening as she gripped my body to hers. She was always on a hairpin trigger to clean up my messes. Always ready to pick up the shattered pieces of whatever I dropped. I wished, while we stood there, that I could stop disappointing her.

"Are you absolutely kidding me?" she suddenly snapped, and I realized her sharp words were directed to the detective and the principal.

"She's a minor. And you were questioning her without a parent present?"

"Ms. Gray, your daughter isn't being detained or questioned," the detective assured my mother. "We were simply asking her if she knew where we might be able to find Miss Frank."

"Madison?" My mom looked at me, her hands going to either side of my face. "Is that who this is about? Something happened to Madison?"

I nodded slowly, feeling the tightness in my throat suddenly melt into a sharp burn, tears welling in my eyes. I hadn't let myself really feel the fear that I'd been holding in my chest. But with my mom looking at me like that, I couldn't hold it off anymore.

"It's okay. I'm sure she's gonna be okay, and I'm sure they"— she glanced darkly at the two other women in the office—"are doing everything they can to make sure she's okay. Yeah?"

I nodded again, blinking big, wet tears down my cheeks, letting my mother brush them away with her fingers.

"I'm taking her home," she declared, adjusting her purse on her shoulder and reaching down to pick up my backpack, shouldering it. "You can call me if you need to speak to her again."

I sniffled and picked up my phone from the desk, shoving it into my back pocket. Vaughn stayed silent, and Morales gave my mother a nod, gesturing toward the open office door.

I didn't break down until I was in the passenger seat of my mom's car. I felt my body folding in on itself, bending and snapping under the weight of what was happening, leaving me a sobbing pile of bones in the front seat. The resolve I had to believe Madison was still alive, waiting for me to find her, wavered and shook, the supports knocked in by the threat of *but what if she's dead?*

As I cried on the drive home, my mom repeated the same quiet refrain, as if she were trying to convince us both.

"It's gonna be okay, baby. Everything's gonna be okay."

Chapter Nineteen

At home, once I'd settled down enough for my mom to feel like she could leave me alone, I curled into the corner of the sofa, my phone cradled on the arm rest. Mom was around the corner in the dining room, talking in a hushed voice on the phone to someone who, I assumed was my aunt. She always turned to her sister when things were going to shit. I could practically hear the anxious hum of Aunt Bee's voice through the phone from the living room.

With Mom no longer hovering, I checked my phone again. I'd gotten a few texts since leaving school. One from Gigi and another from Liam asking if I was okay after he'd heard about Madison. Word had traveled quickly around Willow Creek that Madison Frank was not only missing but possibly dead, and that a photo of her body had been sent to the entire high school. I could almost imagine the club moms, perching themselves on the chaise longues on the pool deck, happy their kids had gone back to school and left them with enough summer to enjoy some afternoons alone. They'd sit there talking over their mai tais, saying how they just *knew* that Frank girl would get herself into trouble.

I had a sudden, visceral urge to burn down the entire club.

Behind me, I heard the back slider open and close as my mom stepped onto the deck, leaving the house fully silent without her hushed speech. I was practically crawling out of my skin to look for Madison, but I didn't even know where to start. It had been hours, and evening was fast approaching. I knew the cops would have been at her house and maybe the club by then. They might even have gone out to the lake house. But that was all too obvious. She wouldn't be in any of those places.

I was drawing a mental map of everywhere we had ever gone together when my phone lit up.

A text from another unknown number.

call this number in 5 minutes for instructions.

All at once, my rib cage seemed to close in on itself. My legs, suddenly riddled with shakes and tremors, unfolded from under me. I quickly stood up, throwing off the blanket I'd pulled over myself. I peeked around the corner, seeing my mom there on the back porch, pacing slowly while she talked.

Every bit of safety and steadiness she'd been working so hard to build for us was about to be shattered by what I was about to do. I knew she'd be terrified, as lost as she'd been while she watched me waste away right in front of her back in Philadelphia.

But I had to do it. I had to see this through and end it.

I shoved my feet into my shoes and snatched my mom's keys from the hook by the door. Quietly, I slipped out the front door and jogged to the RAV4, quickly getting in and starting it. If my mom heard the car start from around back, I had only a few moments before she went inside to investigate and found the couch empty.

I threw the RAV4 in reverse and pulled out, my hands shaking on the wheel as I pushed the gas pedal, headed for the parkway. I checked my phone and saw the clock switch over. My five minutes had passed. I opened the text thread from the unknown number and hit the call button, bringing the phone to my ear. I could hear my pulse thudding loudly against my eardrum as I listened to the phone trill one, two, three times.

And then, a voice.

"Right on time," it said, sick and familiar. "You follow directions so well, Tillie."

"Tell me where the fuck she is, Elliot."

A laugh. I felt my thigh tense, pushing my foot on the gas unintentionally. I quickly slowed, approaching a red light.

"What, you aren't having fun yet? I thought this would be a good game for us to play."

"A game? Are you insane?"

"Not insane, Tillie. Just the wrong person to fuck with."

I gripped the wheel, my knuckles going white. When the light changed, I gunned it.

"You said to call for instructions. So what are they? What do you want me to do?"

"Come join us. We're somewhere you know pretty well. Apparently this has been your and Maddie's little safe space this summer. Fucking creepy, if you ask me."

The only place I could think of hardly made sense. Why would Elliot have Madison there?

"The cemetery? At the lake?"

"Like I said, fuckin' creepy. You have an hour."

The call dropped.

I tossed my phone into the passenger seat and set both hands on the wheel, gripping tightly. I needed to focus on the drive out to the lake and not the now-spiraling thought of how Elliot had known about the cemetery and the playhouse. When we'd first gone there, Madison had sworn she'd never shown that spot to anyone before. Why would she lie?

What else had she lied about?

It took me 48 minutes to speed down the highway toward the exit for Hidden Lake. I tried to stay just above the speed limit, knowing with my luck I'd get stopped for speeding and end up right back where I started, answering stupid questions from the police, who had no idea what was really going on. My phone had rung a hundred times, my mom calling frantically, and I ignored it each time. I knew if I answered, I'd accidentally spill some detail that she'd inevitably latch on to and somehow use to find me. I'd shut off my Life360 and Snap Map and every other possible GPS tracker on my phone; I had even disabled the GPS on the RAV4 menu. I didn't want to be found. I wanted to end this myself.

I took the exit for Hidden Lake and wove my way down the road toward the lake house. But as I pulled up to the turnoff, I thought twice. I couldn't take the boat or park my car there. I had to find another way to the cemetery. I followed the road that wound around the lake, taking another turnoff when I saw a faded, hand-carved sign that read HIDDEN LAKE CEMETERY with an arrow. The clock was ticking down with every extra mile I had to drive, leaving me with hardly four minutes to spare by the time I made it to yet another dirt road that took me deeper into the woods. Where the dirt road dead-ended, I saw Madison's BMW parked in front of a chained-off path.

On the drive to the lake, the sun had set deeper into the sky. Now, as I leapt out of my car and hopped the chain, the woods were darkening quickly, and there was barely enough light dripping through the canopy overhead for me to make my way to the cemetery.

The walk was longer than I needed it to be. I knew my time was almost, if not completely, up when I saw the iron fence appear, the outline of the playhouse finally visible. I pushed my way through the rusted gate and ran to the playhouse, leaves crunching noisily under my steps.

Madison was standing there beside the house, holding her elbows, her limbs visibly shaking. She still had blood in the corner of her mouth, and now I could see the streak of red in her hair had come from a gash on her hairline. It looked painful. It must have been how he'd gotten her into the car.

I wanted to run to her, but she looked at me with wide eyes, shaking her head ever so slightly. As I stepped around the house, I saw Elliot sitting on one of the headstones behind Madison, legs stretched out in front of him, ankles casually crossed. Something in one of his hands caught the light peeking through the trees. He grinned and got to his feet. I saw then what he was holding—a gun. He let it dangle from his fingers, throwing his hands up in mock excitement, that stupid smile still on his face.

"Tillie! How great of you to join us. Now we can really get this soiree started, huh?"

I stepped slowly to the side, my eyes locked on him. I had no idea what his endgame was, but between the gun and wild look in his eye, I wasn't so sure Madison and I would both be leaving alive.

"What do you want, Elliot?" I asked, fighting to keep my voice steady.

He dropped his hands.

"What do I *want*?" he parroted. "I want you and you"— he lifted the gun and pointed it at us in turn as he spoke—"to understand who you're dealing with."

I swallowed hard, feeling like my throat was closing in on

itself. My knees were unsteady, and I watched Madison start to tremble harder, until she had to hold on to the side of the playhouse to keep from falling over.

"I think we've figured it out," I said, taking another step to the side, trying to widen the space between me and Elliot, while stepping closer to Madison.

"We get it. We're sorry. We aren't going to do anything," I quickly added, feeling my voice waver.

Elliot let out a laugh.

"You get it? You're sorry?" he mocked me, shaking his head. "Do you have any idea what Madison here going back on our little deal would mean for me? If you two fucking idiots had managed to use my phone for whatever scheme I'm *sure* you'd cooked up to expose me? I would have lost my spot at Temple. My shot at taking over my dad's firm. My spot on the swim team. My fucking life!"

He yelled the last few words, the deep bellow of his voice nearly knocking me off my feet. I stepped back to catch myself, my legs unsteady. Tears had started streaming down Madison's face.

"All for what, really? For some freshman slut who couldn't keep her mouth shut?" His voice was laced with anger. He stepped in closer.

"Or for you, Maddie? For your little secret about that girl at boarding school? You really proved you'd do anything to keep that from getting out. You, the bitch who'd rather ruin someone's life than admit she's gay? Like it fucking matters?

Well guess what, it doesn't. Nothing about you matters, Maddie. Stop flattering yourself."

Neither Madison nor I spoke. My eyes moved from Elliot to her and back again, my mind racing as I tried to think how to get the gun out of his hand. As if he read my mind, Elliot smirked and stepped over to me, holding the gun between us as he leaned in close, close enough that I could see the sweat beading on his forehead.

"Didn't expect this, did you? Didn't expect me to outsmart you. 'Cause I know you think you're so smart, Tillie Gray. I know more about you than you think."

He paused, taking a step back again, reaching into his back pocket and taking out Madison's phone and showing it to me.

"Or really, she knows a lot about you and wrote it down, so now I do too."

I was trying to unravel his riddle, working through the knots of it in my head. She'd written it down? Written what down?

"How much did you lie to the cops about that girl from your school?"

The ground seemed to drop out from under me. My ears were suddenly filled with the sound of rushing water, the quiet roar of a nighttime ocean, a sharp undercurrent grabbing at my ankles.

"Tillie don't say anything, he doesn't know anything—"

Elliot turned and pointed the gun at Madison, silencing her with one click of the safety. He turned back to me, tossing Madison's phone behind him on the ground.

"I know enough. Enough to open that case wide open again with you in the running for lead suspect. Enough to put you away."

Even if all he knew was what I had lied about, he was right. There had already been eyes on me when Emma first disappeared, some level of suspicion after I'd been the last one to see her, and my flimsy story of having left her swimming alone hadn't really added up all that neatly.

But I knew what he was doing. He was showing me his cards while trying to get me to turn on Madison. He wanted us divided. It would make it easier for him to bargain. Because no matter how big of a shit bag he was, Elliot wasn't going to pull that trigger. He didn't have it in him to clean up the mess.

"Tell me what you want."

He grinned at my words, finally lowering the gun.

"Thatta girl." He stepped toward me again, his grin dropping into a deep scowl. "I want you both to stay the fuck away from me. I want you to go on about your stupid fucking little lives and keep telling the same story that Madison has been telling for a year now. I want you to sing my goddamn praises if anyone ever brings me up, do you hear me?"

I gave him a slow nod, my stomach twisting. I was keenly aware of the way he clicked the safety back on and took his finger off the trigger, the gun still dangling at his side.

"And I don't want you to ever forget that I could destroy you. That I *will* destroy you, if you so much as *think* about changing your mind."

As he finished his threat, Elliot tucked the gun into the back of his pants. I knew it had been a tool to keep us compliant, but once it was out of his hand, I breathed a bit easier.

The sudden smack of one of the newly repaired playhouse shutters against the back of Elliot's head sent him to his knees. The wood splintered when it hit him, cutting into his neck and leaving a trail of red as it dropped behind his shoulders. Madison stood over him, clutching the broken half of the shutter, shaking and staring at me. Her jaw was set, her chest heaving.

The only instinct I had was to step around and snatch the gun from Elliot's back pocket, tossing it off to the side to take it completely out of play. Elliot gripped the back of his head, groaning in pain and anger, and as I moved past him to grab Madison, he hooked an arm around my ankles and knocked them out from under me.

I hit the ground on my back, hard, the air leaving my lungs. I pulled in desperate breaths, rolling onto my side, clutching my middle, trying frantically to breathe. Elliot's hands grabbed for my shoulders, pinning me onto my back, his lumbering frame leaned over me as one of his hands went to my throat, gripping tight.

"That's it!" he was screaming as I gasped for air, writhing under him. "No more negotiating. I'm gonna tell them fucking *everything*, Tillie. And I'll make sure everyone knows what you and Maddie have been covering up together. You're fucking finished, you're—"

Elliot's rant was punctuated by a sudden gasp as his mouth fell open. His grip loosened on me enough that I started to wiggle out from under him, scrambling in the leaves and pine needles until I was out of his reach. He knelt there, hunched over, caught in the middle of trying to breathe, his jaw slack. I watched him reach back behind himself and touch low on his side. When he brought his hand back, it was wet with blood.

Behind Elliot, Madison stood upright, a screwdriver clutched in her hand. Over her trembling shoulder, I saw the playhouse door open, the toolbox we kept inside tipped over out front.

I slowly got to my feet as Elliot sank down to the ground completely, taking quick, small breaths. It took a few long, deafeningly quiet moments for his breaths to stop completely.

The screwdriver dropped from Madison's hand. I stepped over to stand beside her, the both of us looking down at Elliot James, still and quiet at our feet.

"He was never gonna let it go," Madison started, her voice calm but her limbs still trembling. "He would have held everything over our heads forever."

I reached for Madison's hand. She wound her fingers between mine and squeezed tight.

Chapter Twenty

Three days later, the news of Elliot James's disappearance finally broke.

According to the paper, Elliot's parents had reported him missing when he didn't come home from a weekend outing one Sunday night. His Audi was found parked in the back corner of the Starbucks lot on the parkway, nothing inside it. It wasn't until later when Madison had recounted what happened that I learned he'd parked it there himself. He had been waiting in her back seat when she got back to her car with our coffees before picking me up for school. He had the gun, so she listened to him when he told her to drive.

She still hadn't told me all of what took place in those hours between being at Starbucks and me finding them at the cemetery. My mind filled in the blanks with the worst answers it could come up with.

But there were plenty of spaces that didn't need filling in. Too many moments I would relive, awake past dawn, my memory a broken film reel playing on a sickening loop.

Our white-knuckled grip on each of Elliot's wrists as we'd dragged him through the cemetery and through the woods, out of the clearing. The sound of the leaves crunching under our steps as we struggled to pull his body down the narrow path to the dock. The careful movements of our fingers as we unwound the string lights we'd bought to hang on the playhouse and tied loose rocks and broken pieces of old headstones to Elliot's limbs. The quiet huffs of our breaths as we struggled to push him off the end of the dock, his weighted body hitting the water with a noisy *splash*, and then the silence that followed as we knelt on the edge of the splintered dock and watched Elliot disappear from our view.

The way my heart had settled into a slow, even rhythm. My jaw set, my hands steady. And Madison beside me, curling her fingers around my arm and running them down to my hand, holding it in her own. The way we sat there for what felt like hours, days, letting the events settle around us like debris after an explosion, the detonated bomb at the bottom of the lake, a gun tucked into the back of his pants.

The way I watched Madison calmly use the screwdriver to smash Elliot's cell phone into shards, and the way I used the claw end of a hammer to dig a hole in front of Poppy

Holloway's gravestone, burrowing down a foot before we dropped in the phone and the wiped-down screwdriver in and filled the hole back up.

We didn't stop to think if any part of our plan made sense, or what the chances of being caught might be. We moved easily and methodically, two gears in a carefully designed machine.

We stood back and looked at Poppy's grave site, at the playhouse, and I used my foot to brush some leaves back over the patch of dirt we'd disturbed.

"Gotta fix that shutter again," Madison had said as we stood there, and I felt her finger hook into the belt hoop on my jeans, tugging my hip against hers.

When we'd both returned home, dirty and exhausted, it took our parents a few days to shift from grateful and relieved to outright furious.

In an effort to cover up what had really taken place that day, we took the fall for the photo and the text, chalking it up to a poorly planned prank and a bad attempt at ruining our school's ridiculous Welcome Back Week. We told our parents and the cops that everything was staged, and had our cars not gotten stuck in mud outside town, we wouldn't have disappeared for so long. We didn't mean to send our parents into a near frenzy, the cops questioning our friends. Thanks to some hardcore negotiating from our parents and a really well-paid lawyer from Madison's, we both narrowly escaped being charged.

The school held an assembly the next week, berating the entire student body on the dangers of pulling pranks, which quickly devolved into a lecture about not sharing explicit photos and a new school mandate requiring students to leave their cell phones in a designated basket at the start of each class. As if taking our phones during class was really going to mediate the destruction we were so happily and eagerly causing between classes and outside school. As if locking up our devices for fifty minutes at a time was really going to stop us from decimating each other with a single rumor spread through a Snap, a tweet, or a text.

When Elliot was first declared missing, his ever-loyal band of admirers huddled by the lockers in the hallways, smearing their mascara and crying into each other's shoulders, as if he could have remembered any of their names if asked.

And then there was Madison.

Despite the both of us being grounded and essentially barred from spending time together outside school, Madison still found ways to be with me, the most earth-shattering of which happening the day after that assembly. As we walked from the parking lot to the front doors of the school, she reached for my hand. She slid her fingers between mine and held tight, flashing me a grin as we stepped into the building. A few pairs of curious eyes found us as we walked to our respective homerooms, but much to Madison's pleasant surprise, the world didn't implode. The ground didn't fall out from under our feet as we moved through the crowded hallways. Nothing spontaneously burst into flames. Our peers made room for us, giving us space to exist. We knew that the lack of fanfare, good or bad, didn't mean that every pocket of our universe was going to accept this shift. An uneventful walk between classes didn't delude us into believing we could go on existing without friction forever. But it was a start. It was a fire we could warm ourselves with.

The ghosts of what had happened in the wake of Emma's death had tried to haunt me after Elliot, that fearful, dark reminder that even the ultimate sacrifice, even the most extreme steps taken to keep someone you love safe don't always guarantee that that person will still want you when the dust settles. But those ghosts quickly dissipated, as it became more and more clear that if anything, the bond Madison and I had built was only strengthening. The was something powerful about shared secrets. Something that drew us together like moths to a flame, a delicate balance between love and obsession, between safety and destruction. All that girl magic, a pilot light ready to ignite and dissolve us both into ashes at any moment.

Another few weeks into the search for Elliot James, a few of the girls at school planned a candlelight vigil for him. They held it at a park just off the main strip of Willow Creek's tiny downtown district, barely two blocks from where Elliot's car had been parked the night Madison took her car key to the side of it. Neither of our parents questioned us when we asked for a furlough from our sentences to attend the vigil. In fact, my mom drove me to it, dropping me at the park entrance and reaching for my hand before I could get out of the car.

"Hey," she started, then paused, like she was trying to decide the right way to say whatever she was trying to say.

"Are you doing okay?" she finally asked, giving my hand a squeeze.

"Yeah," I said, only a little surprised that I really believed it. "I don't really know Elliot. I just wanna be here to support Madison."

My mom nodded, but she kept her hold on me.

"Right, of course. I just mean...you know. In general. Are you doing okay?"

As I sat there with my other hand on the door, ready to leap out of the car, I realized I hadn't really thought about whether I was doing okay in a larger sense of the word. Really, I hadn't thought much beyond the careful safety of being and remaining in Madison's immediate orbit, both of us dying stars circling one another, caught in each other's gravity. It was such a willing, grateful surrender.

"Yeah." I answered. "Yeah, I'm okay. I'm doing okay. I know I screwed up when school started, and I scared you, but it was...I guess I was still a little mad about having to start over somewhere new."

Even as I shaped the lie in my mouth, I wondered if I was really lying all that much. I still held some resentment about leaving Philly, about moving up to Willow Creek, and for all the shit that had unfolded since we got here. But that resentment could really only, logically, be turned to me. I was the common denominator in all the shitty things that had happened. I was always orchestrating my downfall. Every war I found myself fighting was one I had declared on myself, and one where I was somehow both the ally and the enemy.

My mom smiled and lifted my hand to kiss the back of it before she released her hold. I smiled back and finally opened the car door.

"Have Madison drive you home by nine," she called after me. "I mean it, Til—nine."

"Nine, got it." I playfully saluted her before I bumped the car door shut and wandered into the park. Madison had texted to tell me she was already there, and I quickly spotted her standing near the back of the small group of people who had gathered near the fountain. The girls who had organized the vigil were passing out little candlesticks stuck through the bottoms of waxy paper cups, people sharing their flames to light one another's candles. I stepped up beside Madison and hooked my arm through hers, feeling her clamp it against her side.

"What bullshit," she muttered to me as I was passed a candle. Madison touched her lit wick to mine. "Just a bunch of people trying to draw attention to themselves."

"Isn't that the point of these things?" I asked, my voice as low as hers. "Like how funerals are for the living and not the dead?"

"Yeah, but this isn't that. This is people hoping to find a guy who did nothing but cause harm when he was here. There's no way that all these people genuinely want him to turn back up."

I knew that at least two people there didn't want him to return, but those two people knew with absolute certainty that he wouldn't. I squeezed my arm around Madison's, and she flashed her eyes at me.

"If this is people trying to draw attention to themselves," I whispered to her, watching the light from her candle shadow her face. "Then why did we come?"

Madison's mouth curled into a smirk, and I felt that fire in my belly flare, the heat rising into my chest.

"Because, Tillie," she said softly, "appearances are everything around here. And besides, watching people cosplay grief amuses me."

There was something so self-assured and certain in her voice that it made me feel safe and untouchable. I turned my attention to the girl who had stepped up onto a bench a few yards ahead and was addressing the group. It was Sienna, her hair now in long braids that fell over her shoulders, her face serious and mouth set in a frown.

"We're all here to pray for the safe return of Elliot James," she began, raising her voice enough to quiet the conversations among those who had gathered. "Elliot is a fixture in Willow Creek, a legacy, an accomplished athlete and student. We hope he is safe and will return to his friends and family."

While Sienna spoke, I looked over at Madison. She pressed

her lips together, like she was fighting a smile. The thrill of our secret sent a wave of exhilaration through my limbs, and I felt my own lips daring to curl into a smile. Madison caught my eye, and we both had to bite our lips from laughing.

We were invincible, Madison and me. Even as we stood with two dropped bodies between us, we were alight with all that girl magic, happily caught in a spell we'd eagerly cast on each other.

"You know," Madison said softly to me, "it only seems fair that your friend Greer faces some consequences too."

Madison looked at her candle, watching the wax drip down into the cup, turning and tilting it in her hand. "People shouldn't get away with hurting us."

She looked at me again.

Before I could process her words, I was nodding. She was right. We were powerful enough then, I knew, to destroy anyone who wronged us. And Greer's name had moved to the top of that list.

As I started mulling over the best ways to find a weakness in Greer's armor, Madison leaned over and pressed her lips to mine. I kissed her back, a moment passing before I remembered where we were. But she pressed harder into the kiss, moving her arm around my waist to draw me in, only breaking our kiss when I could sense at least a few pairs of eyes on us.

She gave me a smile, then turned her attention forward, setting her mouth into a charade of seriousness, putting on her best attempt at a frown.

My heart rattled in my chest.

As the group began to disperse, Madison blew out her candle and stepped aside.

"I'm gonna go play normalcy and say hi to them," she said, gesturing vaguely to her group of friends. "I'll be right back."

I watched her walk away, the circle of girls she had called friends eagerly opening to welcome her inside, ever willing her to reclaim her rightful seat on the throne. I watched as she feigned sadness with them, hugging each girl in a tight embrace, no doubt exchanging condolences and wishes for Elliot's safe return. She played the role like a practiced actor, and none of the girls seemed to second-guess it.

My phone vibrated in my back pocket.

I tugged it out and saw a notification for a text from an unknown number. Instinctively my insides twisted.

I opened the message.

madison isn't who you think she is.

I looked up from my phone and scanned the group, looking for anyone else with a phone in their hand. No one was actively texting or even holding their phones. Most of them were still engaged in quiet conversations. As I frantically searched the park with my eyes, my phone vibrated again.

A link appeared in the text feed. I tapped it, and my browser opened an article from a newspaper based in Poughkeepsie, New York. The headline at the top of the page read *Student Found Dead at Poughkeepsie Boarding School.*

A fifteen-year-old sophomore at Walden Preparatory Boarding School in Poughkeepsie was found dead after an apparent overdose on Sunday evening. Police have ruled the death accidental, and representatives from the school have indicated a push toward ensuring student safety through mandatory drug screens and searches.

Daisy's name rose into the center of my chest like a brick of lead. This was the story I'd been keeping myself from unraveling. This was the secret Madison had been willing to defend Elliot over, the one she was so scared of that she thought the only way to keep it quiet had been to kill him.

Another text notification popped up on my screen from the unknown number. I opened the message and found another link, this time to an Instagram post—one of Madison's I'd seen weeks before. The photo of her and Daisy grinning on the picnic table in their school uniforms, the caption reading: will be missing this smile forever. my heart is in pieces. love you always.

I could hear blood rushing past my ears. I looked up to see Madison still schmoozing with the group of friends she had called fake and boring the first time we'd spoken.

I remembered what she had said to me that day at the playhouse, recounting how she'd ended up with Elliot. *Ever since I got back from boarding school, she'd said, I've fought for my fucking life to fit the mold, to look and act how everyone wants me to so that I don't have to deal with the fallout.*

Elliot's words in the cemetery surfaced next—*your little secret about that girl at boarding school? You really proved you'd do anything to keep that from getting out.*

It felt like gravity was shifting around me, making me heavier and weightless all at once, my heart racing wildly behind my rib cage. I let the hand holding my phone drop down to my side, the screen going black as I stood there watching Madison, my mind filling in the blanks with the worst, but still refusing to believe anything bad about her, even after watching her tie rocks to her ex-boyfriend's body and emotionlessly push him into a lake. If I had to believe bad things about her, I had to also believe them about myself.

Madison finally untangled herself from the girls and walked back to me, a smile crossing her face as she locked her eyes on mine. I could practically feel the rush of uncertainty fighting the visceral need I had for her, right in the center of me.

"Hey," she said, reaching over to take my burned-out candle from my other hand, tossing it into the nearby trash can. "You ready to head home?"

As I studied her, re-memorizing the curves of her face and the way a lock of blond hair had delicately fallen over one of her eyes, I tried to imagine a universe where I didn't love her. Where I wouldn't lay down my entire existence to protect hers. I was coming up empty.

Madison offered me her hand.

"Yeah," I said, lacing my fingers between hers. "I'm ready."

Acknowledgments

Thank you endlessly to my agent Sharon for being the best support system a sophomore writer could ever ask for. Thank you to the absolutely phenomenal team at Sourcebooks Fire, including Annie and Annette, for your guidance and for believing in me and in Tillie.

To Lindy, my biggest cheerleader and best friend, this book wouldn't exist without you and your tireless support. I will be forever grateful for how fortunate I was to tumble into your life, and how lucky I am to remain a part of it.

To my family: Mom, Dad, Michael, Christopher, Catherine, Danielle, thank you for being the best fan club in the world. Your support and love are unmatched.

To everyone who read and loved *The Violent Season*, I hope you love Tillie and Madison with the same depth as you loved

Wyatt and Porter. Thank you for being the reason I got to write the sapphic thriller of my dreams.

Writing this book was one of the most challenging things I have ever done in my life. I wrote it while working full-time serving victims and survivors of sexual and domestic violence. Working as an advocate and dedicating my time and energy to providing support and safety to those folks is the most rewarding thing I have the privilege of doing, and without the things I learned from those experiences, I don't think the stories and characters in this book would be as authentic as I hope they are. As a survivor of sexual assault myself, I hope anyone who reads this book and may be a survivor knows they aren't alone. Help is available.

You are important. Your experiences are valid. You are deserving of respect and love. And I believe you.

About the Author

Sara Walters works as an advocate for victims and survivors of domestic and sexual violence in central Pennsylvania. Previously, she worked as a reproductive rights advocate and a college instructor. She earned her MFA in creative writing at the University of South Florida and studied children's and young adult literature while earning her doctorate in education at the University of Tennessee. She believes in the power of storytelling as a voice for survivors and aims to give space to the stories too often silenced.

HELP AND RESOURCES

National Sexual Assault Hotline
1-800-656-4673

The Trevor Project
https://www.thetrevorproject.org/get-help/

To Write Love on Her Arms
https://twloha.com/find-help/

FIREreads

Ⓢ #getbooklit

Your hub for the hottest in young adult books!

Visit us online and sign up for our
newsletter at FIREreads.com

 @sourcebooksfire

 sourcebooksfire

 firereads.tumblr.com